The Kharakternyks.

The Legacy of Sarmatian Seers

RUSLAN BIEDOV

2025

Copyright © 2025 RUSLAN BIEDOV

All rights reserved

The characters and events portrayed in this book are fictitious. Any similarity to real persons, living or dead, is coincidental and not intended by the author. No part of this book may be reproduced, or stored in a retrieval system, or transmitted in any form or by any means, electronic, mechanical, photocopying, recording, or otherwise, without express written permission of the publisher.

ISBN: 9798305581911

Imprint: Independently published

Cover design by: Volodymyr Evkar, Ruslan Biedov

Translated from Ukrainian by Ruslan Biedov

Printed in the United States of America

"Those who are swift and cunning, able to find their way through any challenge, are given by their comrades the title of kharakternyk—a kind of superhuman whom bullets cannot harm and who can saddle even the devil himself, forcing him to serve." Yevhen Hrebinka.

Prologue

In a roadside tavern on the edge of a small village, lost amidst the endless steppe, the post-afternoon hours bustled with life. Having finished their work, local farmers sat back. They sipped the strong mead brewed by Theophil, the rotund, aging tavern keeper. His name wasn't remarkable. But most villagers owed him money, so they called him "Jew" though Theophil was very offended by it.

Theophil, the owner of the last tavern in the Southern Steppe untouched by Tatar's[1] raids, was a widower. He knew almost the entire Psalter by heart. His fourteen-year-old son dreamed of joining the Sich[2] to "slay Poles and infidels" but he feared his father too much to act on it.

---

[1] Crimean Tatars are an indigenous people of Crimea. Their formation occurred during the 13th–17th centuries, primarily from Cumans that appeared in Crimea in the 10th century.

[2] Sich(Ukrainian:ciч), was an administrative and military center of the Zaporozhian Cossacks. The word *sich* derives from the Ukrainian verb "to chop" – with the implication of clearing a forest for an encampment or of building a fortification with the trees that have been chopped down. The Zaporozhian Sich was the fortified capital of the Zaporozhian Cossacks, located on the Dnipro, in the 16th–18th centuries in the Ukraine.

The tavern's most awaited guests were the salt merchants from Perekop[3]. Their low, creaking wagons carried salt and an array of wares for trade on the dusty square before the modest yet well-kept chapel. These fairs made the villagers long for the merchants' seasonal journeys.

No one had expected the man in Cossack attire who appeared in the doorway that day. Sich warriors weren't welcomed here. People feared that Tatar horsemen might herald their arrival, which, by God's grace, they hadn't seen in years.

The Cossack shut the door, crossed himself before the icon, and bowed low. He removed his hat, greeted the patrons, and then approached the innkeeper.

"Water and hay for my horse, and a glass of mead for myself," he said with a courteous tone.

Theophil eyed the guest, then called for his son to tend to the horse. Pouring a full glass, he placed it on the counter. The Cossack paid immediately, taking a sip without sitting. The long road and two sleepless nights created a heavy burden for him.

Upon seeing the coins, the innkeeper's demeanor softened.

"How fares the Sich?" he asked, offering a sycophantic smile. "Does the Holy Mother of God still shield her knights and their fortress?"

---

[3] The Isthmus of Perekop, literally Isthmus of the Trench (Ukrainian: Перекопський перешийок) is the narrow,(3.1–4.3 mi) wide strip of land that connects the Crimean Peninsula to the mainland of Ukraine. ↑

"I wouldn't know," the stranger replied. "I haven't been there since last month's new moon."

"Ah, I see," Theophil murmured. He refrained from asking for more. "When was the last time infidels passed through here?" asked the Cossack.

The innkeeper rushed to make the sign of the cross.

"Not since Catherine's Day…"

The Cossack nodded silently, sitting at a dark corner table with a fresh glass of mead. Moments later, the patrons, as if on cue, seemed to forget the stranger's presence.

When the last, drunken guests had staggered home, the innkeeper's son was about to bolt the tavern door with its heavy iron latch. At that moment, two Tatars appeared in the doorway. They carried sabers and tucked pistols into wide leather belts.

Theophil's heart raced, but he concealed his fear. Beneath the counter, he had a loaded pistol ready for such moments, though he prayed it wouldn't come to that. He suspected their purpose and even hoped to earn some coin for valuable information.

"We're looking for a Cossack," one of the Tatars said, stepping inside with a look of open disdain on his round, ruddy face, while his companion scanned the room.

"Murza[4] Haji Bey is eager to meet him," the first added, "but it seems we've missed him."

---

[4] Murza is an aristocratic title in Ottaman Empire.

"There was one here," the innkeeper admitted, careful to keep his eyes on the dangerous visitors. "He drank three glasses and left."

The Tatars exchanged curious glances and stepped closer.

"Did you see which way he went?" one asked.

Theophil was about to say the Cossack[5] had mounted his horse and headed northwest, toward the Fortress. In truth, neither he, his son, nor anyone else had seen where the man had gone. He disappeared. But where else would he go? Surely to the Island Fortress. Why not share this guess, especially if it might earn him a little Tatar silver? But that evening, Theophil had no chance to profit from his knowledge. His mouth opened and his eyes bulged as he stared at fearsome creature emerged from the shadowy doorway behind the Tatars.

---

[5] Ukrainian Cossacks were nomads who led a military lifestyle and earned their livelihood through war and crafts (hunting, fishing, later trade, and agriculture). These people participated in military campaigns and were part of the state troops or outside guards of wealthy people.

PART ONE

Ivan Rudyi

Chapter One

The Ukrainian hamlet spread across the gentle hills of the high Vorskla Riverbank. Whitewashed huts gleamed like pearls amidst a green sea of tidy orchards, melon fields, gardens, and meadows. The sun was high. A drowsy, hot stillness blanketed the world. It lulled everything into a sweet, midday slumber. Only an occasional discontented "moo" from a cow or the droning hum of a beetle in the warm air broke the silence.

In the spacious yard of old Mykola Sobol, everything seemed lifeless. Even the usually noisy geese quietly fussed around a large puddle in the clearing near the fence.

The clatter of pots broke the silence. It was Sobol's wife bustling about. After tidying up, she began to grumble. As usual, she directed her complaints at her husband, who still hadn't repaired the fence along the property line after more than a week. The neighbor's chickens took their turn by raiding the melon patch the previous evening, a surprise to everyone. Lastly, she turned her ire toward Petro, the youngest son of old Sobol.

"Where is that scoundrel, I'd like to know!" She muttered irritably while rummaging through the huge, iron-bound chest. It took up a third of the small parlor. "Does he even care that the livestock needs watering?"

"He doesn't even have a mustache yet to care with," joked old Sobol, turning over on his side. His wife's muttering had woken him back when she was ranting about the neighbor's chickens. As for the fence, he either didn't hear or pretended not to. Fixing the fence meant dealing with Ivan Kozhemyaka, the neighbor. Sobol didn't like him. He secretly dabbled in usury and had dealings with the Poles.

"And you don't care that our cows will die from thirst, do you?" Sobol's wife snapped, seizing the opportunity to have her husband's ear. "Are you useless blind log? That lazy good-for-nothing of a son has completely gone wild! He doesn't listen to me! All he does is chase girls at evening gatherings!"

"He should be off to the Sich," Sobol said dreamily, letting out a sigh. "Let him follow in the footsteps of his brother, Stepan."

His wife froze for a moment, then glared at him with wide eyes. "Have you completely lost your mind?" she thundered. Sobol instantly regretted mentioning the Sich. "Are you insane, you shameless cripple? Wasn't it enough that you lost your arm there? Wasn't it enough that your eldest, Stepan, died at the hands of the infidels? And now you want Petro to follow him?"

"Calm down, woman," Sobol's voice grew stern. "You'd rather my sons hide under your skirts, twisting cow tails and shoveling dung. But the fact that Poles and infidels destroy our Orthodox people, steal our goods, and drag our daughters into captivity doesn't matter to you, does it? Typical woman!"

With that, Sobol stood and, with a practiced motion, tucked his empty right sleeve into the wide red sash of his Cossack belt. "Instead of babbling about things you don't understand, you'd be better off cooking something to eat."

For a moment, Sobol's wife stared at him as if she'd seen a ghost. Then she opened her mouth, drawing in a deep breath to deliver a scathing retort, but before she could, the sound of hooves reached their ears from outside. Startled, she clasped her hands together. "Could it be the Poles?" she whispered.

Sobol peered through the small window overlooking the yard but saw nothing. The hoofbeats had already faded. "I told you to negotiate with Kozhemyaka!" she snapped again, this time in a hiss. "Now he's sent the Poles after us! What will you do now?"

A knock at the door interrupted them. Sobol's wife crossed herself and began muttering a prayer under her breath, her eyes fixed on the door as if it were a specter.

"Why are you standing there, silly woman? Look who it is!" Sobol growled, darting toward the stove where he kept his saber and pistol.

"Go yourself," she retorted. "This is your doing. What have I done to deserve such punishment?"

The knock came again, louder this time.

"Anybody home or has everyone died here?" called the visitor.

"May you burn in hell, you cursed..." Sobol's wife muttered as she crossed herself in a hurry before the icons in the corner.

Sobol dropped his weapon in the middle of the room and ran to open the door.

"You're worse than any Pole, old hag!" he bellowed cheerfully. "You'd scare anyone off with your nagging. It's Ivan Rudyi visiting me, my old friend!"

In the doorway stood a towering figure of a Cossack, a full head taller than Sobol. He wore wide, mud-streaked crimson trousers made of fine Turkish cloth. His sweat-drenched shirt clung to his body, and a saber hung at his side, with two pistols tucked into his belt. The two old comrades embraced.

"Looks like you've turned into a proper dumpling under that wife's skirt, Sobol! Your bellies are as round as a pig's, and your face is no better!" Rudyi teased.

Sobol waved him off with a laugh and invited him to the table under the straw canopy by the house.

"Woman," he called into the house, "bring some mead for our guest!"

"That guest is worse than a Pole," she muttered under her breath but went to fetch the mead.

The two Cossacks sat down, sharing memories and laughter as the shadows of evening slowly enveloped the hamlet.

Chapter Two

"Somebody told me that Sirko[6] keeps the devil himself as his servant. Is it true, or just a tale?" Petro asked, watching Ivan Rudyi sharpening his saber, wiping it with a cloth.

"And they also say," Petro continued, "that neither infidels nor Poles can defeat Sirko because dark forces are on his side."

"People lie about his invincibility," Ivan replied while checking his pistols. "And the talk of dark forces? Pure nonsense. They speak of what they neither know nor understand. Don't believe them."

"Well, I'd like to be like Sirko…" Petro mused aloud.

"Petro!" came a sharp voice from the house. "Where are you loafing? Have you fed the geese yet?"

"What's the matter?" Rudyi asked with a smirk.

"My mother can't even bear to hear about the Sich," Petro sighed. "Three days before you arrived, I asked my father to let me practice swinging his saber in the yard. When my mother saw it, she

---

[6] Ivan Sirko (Ukrainian: Іван Сірко, 1605 – 1680) was a Zaporozhian Cossack military leader, Koshovyi Otaman of the Zaporozhian Host and putative co-author of the famous semi-legendary-Cossack-letter-to the Ottoman sultan that inspired the major painting Reply of the Zaporozhian Cossacks by the 19th-century artist Ilya Repin. ↑

snatched it away and gave me a good beating with the hilt. She scolded me terribly. Father says it's because my older brother Stepan died at the hands of the infidels."

"Yes, he died. And what about it? As if one can't meet the same end here," Ivan replied.

"But the infidels are far away…"

"Not so far as you think, boy. If every Cossack hides behind his fence, too afraid of death to act, the infidels will come here sooner or later. And trust me, the Poles won't stay quiet for long. Khmelnytskyi[7] struck them hard, but not hard enough. So, tell me—who will defend this land if not us?"

"You're right," Petro said in a gentle tone. "But my mother is very stubborn in her opposition to the Sich." Even my father can't change her mind."

"Your father has grown old and weak; that's why he can't," Rudyi replied.

"Uncle Ivan," Petro said after a pause, "are you going hunting now?"

"Hunting?" Rudyi grinned. "You could call it that. Why?"

"I'd like to go with you, Uncle Ivan," Petro said dreamily.

---

[7] The Khmelnytsky Uprising, also known as the Cossack–Polish War, was a Cossack rebellion that took place between 1648 and 1657 in the eastern territories of the Polish Lithuanian Commonwealth, which led to the creation of a Cossack Hetmanate in Ukraine. Under the command of hetman Bohdan Khmelnytskyi, the Zaporozhian Cossacks fought against Polish domination and Commonwealth's forces

"And what about the geese and cows?" Rudyi asked, giving the boy a sly look.

"The geese? I'll handle them in an hour, and then we can go. I'll tell my father I'm going hunting with you. That is if you don't mind…"

"He must be a good Cossack," Rudyi thought to himself. Aloud, he said uncertainly, "I don't know what to say…"

"Please, Uncle Ivan!" Petro pleaded. "I'll carry all the spoils back myself. I'll do whatever you say!"

"Alright then. Go saddle your father's mare," Rudyi instructed, deciding not to wait for the boy to offer him the moon. "I'll wait by the river in the ravine with my horse."

Petro dropped whatever he had in his hands and dashed off to fulfill the order. Rudyi adjusted his topknot, twirled his mustache with satisfaction, and set off toward the ravine with his horse.

The sun had risen above the sharp treetops and was beginning to scorch the land. Petro caught up with Rudyi on his father's mare.

"Hurry up, boy," Rudyi called impatiently. "By noon, we need to be fifteen versts southwest of Poltava."

"Zirka is tired," Petro replied. "Father never pushes her this hard or this far."

"Your father has ruined the poor beast by keeping her penned up all the time. Fine. Let's rest for a moment, but we'll need to move quickly afterward. We're short on time."

"I thought we were going hunting," Petro said as he dismounted and led the mare into the shade of a sprawling ash tree. "How can we hunt if we've left the forest behind?"

"Our prey isn't in that forest," Rudyi said cryptically.

"Don't tell me we're going after Poles, just the two of us?" Petro asked, his curiosity piqued.

"Not to fight them, not yet," Rudyi replied, leaping onto his horse and signaling for Petro to do the same. "But if it comes to that, we'll be ready."

Petro realized that Rudyi was keeping something from him but didn't dare press for answers.

It was well past noon when Rudyi finally halted his weary horse in a grove near a sandy riverbank. Exhausted from the heat, Petro dismounted. He tied the mare to a slender hornbeam and collapsed into the fragrant tall grass.

"Hard day, Petro?" Rudyi asked with a grin.

"Is this what it means to be a Cossack?" Petro muttered, dripping with sweat. "To drive yourself and your horse to the death?"

"That depends on the Cossack," Rudyi replied with a cunning smile.

Petro lifted his head and studied Rudyi. Something about him seemed strange. At first, Petro couldn't put his finger on it, but then it hit him: Rudyi didn't look tired at all, as though he'd spent the entire day lounging in the shade. And why hadn't the blazing sun scorched his shaven head with its silver tuft of hair?

"Did you sell your soul to the devil, Uncle Ivan, so he'd shield you from the heat?" Petro asked with a hint of suspicion.

Rudyi burst into laughter and pulled out his pipe. "What would the devil want with my soul?" he chuckled. "The sun's no great trouble!"

"So too," Petro agreed. "But if a man rides thirty versts without breaking a sweat, there must be some dark magic at work."

"I told you, boy, the devil has nothing to do with it," Rudyi replied, lighting his pipe. "But there is an art to it—learning not to fear the blazing sun, the biting cold, or an enemy's bullet."

"Teach me that art, Uncle Ivan!" Petro exclaimed, his eyes wide with wonder.

"You're a sharp one, Sobol's son," Rudyi replied with a chuckle. "Eager to learn everything, and all at once!"

"I'll do whatever you ask! Just teach me not to fear the heat or enemy bullets so I can fight the infidels!"

"First, go water the horses and rest," Rudyi said with a smile.

"But why are we here?" Petro dared to ask.

"Those who know too much often end up with little," Rudyi replied, disappearing into the curling smoke of his pipe.

Chapter Three

Petro awoke in the dead of night. The sky was shrouded in heavy clouds, and Rudyi was nowhere to be seen. The horses snorted nervously, sensing the approach of a storm.

Young Sobol tried to recall when he had fallen asleep. After watering the horses, he had lain down in the grass to rest briefly, talking to Rudyi about his life. Rudyi had shared stories about fighting Poles with Petro's father under Khmelnytskyi[8] They had advanced as far as Lviv. Then... Petro must have drifted off. Yet this sleep had been different—deep and unnaturally heavy, unlike anything he had experienced, even on his most exhausting days. Could that cunning *kharakternyk*[9] have bewitched him? But why?

---

[8] The Khmelnytsky Uprising, also known as the Cossack–Polish War, was a Cossack rebellion that took place between 1648 and 1657 in the eastern territories of the Polish Lithuanian Commonwealth, which led to the creation of a Cossack Hetmanate in Ukraine. Under the command of hetman Bohdan Khmelnytskyi, the Zaporozhian Cossacks fought against Polish domination and Commonwealth's forces. ↑

[9] In Ukrainian folklore, a kharakternyk is a powerful sorcerer and warrior who was either born with such a gift or has learned to be one from others. Usually, only Cossacks were called kharakternyks. Animals, and birds obey them. They could turn into wolves, falcons, and hounds. They have the gift of hypnotizing people and finding treasures. They can communicate with witches, devils, and ghouls, but they do not harm people. ↑

Petro glanced around. Along the gentle eastern riverbank stretched the steppe. The river brought a pleasant coolness. The wind rustled the treetops and played with fragrant grasses. Petro decided to refresh himself. Approaching the water, he noticed lights on the high bank across the river. They were close, but the night and wind obscured what was happening. Large, cold raindrops began to drum against his back. But Petro didn't hesitate, he dove into the dark, rain-dimpled water and swam to the opposite shore.

The storm raged for only a few minutes. The angry sky crashed down on the parched earth, and then it settled into a stillness. The wind scattered the remaining clouds, and silence fell. Climbing up the clay slope, Petro crept close to the source of the lights. As he approached, he heard voices—one belonged to Rudyi, while the other clearly spoke Polish.

"If the esteemed lord truly recognizes him as the leader of the Zaporizhian Host, then why does he refuse to negotiate with his representative?" Rudyi's voice was calm and measured.

"Lord Stotsky does respect Sirko as a warrior and a diplomat," the Pole said in a hushed falsetto. "But Sirko does not respect Lord Stotsky." Otherwise, the ataman would have come to the talks himself."

"But the esteemed lord, who represents His Majesty the King, also did not attend, sending his adjutant instead," Rudyi countered. "I believe I've proven to you that I am who I claim to be. Let us dispense with formalities and get to the matter at hand."

"His Majesty, the King, has a proposal for the atamans of the Zaporizhian Host," the Polish envoy said, his irritation barely concealed. "His Majesty does not wish the Hetmanate's alliance with the Tsar of Moscow to hinder the Sich's development of amicable relations with the Commonwealth. Such relations could be mutually beneficial."

"The Sich is always willing to hear advantageous proposals from the King," Rudyi replied. "But why the secrecy?"

"There are matters best discussed in whispers," the Pole retorted, growing more annoyed.

"Then let's get to the point," Rudyi said, his tone unchanged.

"The borders of the Commonwealth have recently suffered from Turkish incursions. The Sultan seeks to expand his territories into our lands. Europe tempts the Ottomans as honey attracts a fly. His Majesty knows well the vast experience of the Zaporizhian Cossacks in fighting Tatars and Turks. A strike on the fortress of Kazykermen[10] could distract the Sultan from European affairs. Naturally, such help would be generously compensated. I believe His Majesty's gift will serve as a persuasive argument for the ataman and his warriors."

With that, the envoy placed a heavy leather pouch before Rudyi.

In the darkness, bushes rustled, and a loud commotion erupted.

---

[10] Kyzy-Kermen (Kazykermen) fortress was built on the site of present-day Beryslav. According to chronicles, it was the strongest fortification in the entire lower Dnipro area.

"What's going on?" Rudyi asked grimly. "Did the esteemed lord fail to keep his word and bring soldiers?"

In the firelight, the Pole's face turned pale, resembling that of a corpse. He shot Rudyi a glare.

"Who do you take me for?!" the envoy hissed. "I kept my word. I brought no soldiers, though I have my guards with me—as is my right. But it seems you've not shed your spying habits!"

"What nonsense are you spouting?" Rudyi snapped, springing to his feet. "I came alone. You're the one who's set a trap for me!"

"Oh, really?" the Pole sneered. "Let's see about that. Perhaps it's just an animal wandering in the dark." He gestured toward the shadows. Two soldiers emerged, dragging Petro with his hands bound behind his back.

"Is this not your 'animal,' Master Rudyi?" the Pole asked with a mocking tone. "You'll tell me how many more lurk in the dark, waiting for the chance to rob a noble lord?"

"That's no animal," Rudyi said with relief upon seeing Petro. "That's... my squire. I, too, am entitled to one."

The envoy's thin brows shot up to his furrowed forehead.

"A squire without a weapon?" he asked coldly, taking Petro's chin between two fingers and studying his frightened face.

"Why is your squire unarmed, then?" he asked, his voice now calm and measured.

Chapter Four

They rode back at a slow pace, in silence. Each man lost himself in his own thoughts. Rudyi, his thick brows streaked with gray, furrowed in anger, stared straight ahead. His right hand rested on his saber's hilt. His knotted, dirt-under-the-nails fingers traced the ridges of the grip. A surge of anxiety washed over him. The Cossack radiated pure fury. It made anyone think twice about approaching him.

Petro followed his father on the mare, staying a short distance behind. He didn't dare speak to Rudyi, fully aware of the trouble he'd caused. Shame burned within him—he had let down the Cossack who had trusted him! If his father found out, a lash would follow, but that wasn't what worried Petro now. He wanted to atone for his guilt to Rudyi, even if it meant enduring the harshest punishment. The last thing he wanted was for Rudyi to think he was not only a fool but also a coward.

When they finally stopped to water the horses, Petro summoned the courage to speak.

"Uncle Ivan," he began hesitantly.

"What?" Rudyi asked, glancing at Petro as if seeing him for the first time.

"I just wanted to say about what happened..."

"Eh!" Rudyi cut him off with an irritated wave of his hand. "What could you say? A foolish head makes for tired legs!"

There was no malice in Rudyi's voice, which left Petro feeling even more confused.

"Still, to fail like that..." Petro muttered, ashamed. Rudyi turned to him.

"You want to become a true Cossack—one whom neither bullet nor enemy blade can harm? Have you changed your mind?"

"Of course not, Uncle Ivan!" Petro's eyes lit with youthful fire. "I'm the son of a Cossack, and I want to be one too! Please don't be angry with me—I'll never..."

"Then don't tell your father what happened," Rudyi interrupted him. "If he finds out, he won't let you go to the Sich with me. And, in truth, he'd be right, I, the old fool, came close to losing his last child today! Let this be a lesson for me as well. And you, boy, keep your nose out of trouble, or one day you might lose not only your nose but your head too. Don't test a Cossack's fate for no reason—it serves greater purposes."

"Yes, Uncle Ivan..." Petro replied, surprised by the sudden shift in Rudyi's tone.

"So, are you ready to start learning the ways of the Cossacks?" Rudyi asked with a twinkle in his eye, as if nothing had happened. Petro nearly leaped out of his saddle.

"I want to walk through walls like Sirko does!" he exclaimed, then hesitated under Rudyi's amused gaze. "At least, that's what they say…"

Rudyi approached and looked Petro squrely in the eyes. "Don't listen to idle chatter. Walk your own path."

"So, what should I do, Uncle?" Petro asked eagerly. Rudyi dismounted, stepping onto the roadside, and gestured to the distance.

"Do you see that hill with the spruce tree on top?"

"Of course."

"Take this stone and place it by the tree before the midday heat sets in."

Petro inspected the stone, walking around it before removing his jacket and hefting it onto his shoulders. The rock felt light, and the hill had a slight slope. Confident, Petro decided he could easily handle the task.

"Quickly now," Rudyi urged. "The sun is already high!" A keen eye might have caught the faint trace of irony hidden in Rudyi's thick mustache.

Petro silently shouldered the stone and jogged toward the hill. At first, his legs carried him with ease, and he felt confident he would reach the summit well ahead of noon. But as the incline grew steeper, his shoulder began to ache unbearably. He paused to rest under a small hornbeam, regretting that he hadn't brought any water. After chewing on a few juicy dandelions, Petro glanced at the blue sky. The blazing sun, as if mocking him, seemed to rush toward its zenith faster than usual.

Grasping the stone once more, Petro climbed step by step. The slope was much steeper than it had appeared from a distance. He focused on each movement: one step—good; another step—better. He refused to think about the searing pain where the sharp edges of the rock dug into his body.

Exhausted, Petro collapsed onto the ground, gasping for air. He felt as if he might soon meet his end—and not in some grand Cossack battle, but here, on this damned hill. He no longer cared whether he reached the top in time.

A branch cracked nearby. Petro turned his stiff neck to see Rudyi sprawled on a pile of hay beneath a viburnum bush, calmly polishing his saber with a clean cloth.

"If I were your enemy, you'd already be dead," Rudyi said, studying the boy with a discerning gaze. What he saw didn't please him.

"How did you get here?" Petro asked, then smiled weakly. "Of course, you have your horse..." Rudyi shrugged, sheathing his saber with a single precise motion.

"My horse is tied to the willow next to yours," Rudyi said. "And you didn't make it to the top—look, the suns at its peak." Petro glanced at Rudyi in frustration, then turned to see that he was just a dozen steps from the summit.

"Imagine that instead of a stone, you were carrying weapons and ammunition for your comrades," Rudyi continued. "They needed it immediately, not a moment later. If you're late, many people die—because you couldn't make it in time."

Petro dropped his gaze.

"Uncle Ivan..." he began to protest but fell silent under Rudyi's stern look.

"You're not a Cossack yet, Petro," Rudyi said coldly, examining his ornate pistol.

The words pierced Petro's heart. What kind of man was he? His father had fought infidels and Poles; his brother had died defending their land. And him? What was he, other than a boy who herded geese and chased after girls?

"But I'll speak to your father," Rudyi said after a pause. "I think he'll let me make a man out of you."

"Thank you, Uncle Ivan," Petro said, his voice trembling with a mix of relief and determination. But Rudyi raised his hand to stop him.

"Don't thank me. Just pick up that stone and follow me to the top of the hill."

In an instant, Petro forgot his exhaustion. He grabbed the stone and hurried after Rudyi.

Rudyi waited at the hill's summit, gazing at the horizon. Petro straightened to his full height and stood beside him.

"Isn't that your village by the river, beyond those woods?" Rudyi asked softly, his voice so low that Petro barely heard him. At that moment, the hot, viscous air was disrupted by a sudden gust carrying the acrid scent of burnt wood.

"Someone must be burning a bonfire," Petro thought. Aloud, he said,

"Yes, that's my village. Maybe someone slaughtered a pig…"

"That's too much black smoke for a pig," Rudyi murmured, his tone making Petro's stomach tighten with dread.

Indeed, dark clouds were rising over the forest, spreading like sinister black tentacles.

"What is it, Uncle?" Petro asked, alarmed. "Don't ask me, boy," Rudyi said, placing a hand on his saber's hilt. "Just run to your horse."

They descended the hill in silence. A slow, sickening sense of dread began to grow in Petro's chest, the same feeling he'd had when news of his brother's death had reached their home.

Chapter Five

The wooden, well-kept chapel stood tall on a small hill beyond the last row of houses on the village's edge. The old cemetery with its humble crosses was visible from a distance. So was the aging priest's low-roofed house. When Petro was very young, he and his brother would spy on the priest. They saw him sneak off during the day to buy mead from the Jewish tavern keeper. The tavern stood along the Kyiv Road, not far from the cemetery. The village women considered this lone tavern cursed. They used its bad reputation to frighten their husbands, who were drawn there like flies to filth.

From a distance, the chapel and the tavern blazed with equal intensity. The villagers murmured that one was sacred while the other was sinful. Thick smoke poured into the overcast sky. It lingered in the heavy, gelatinous air, stretching out its inky fingers toward a shadowy cloud rolling in from the northeast. Concealed among the trees, Rudyi and Petro found silence. They saw no houses and heard no sounds. It was as if the world beyond had vanished.

Overhead, the tall ash tree rustled its parched leaves with an unusually loud and ominous whisper. Petro barely stood on his trembling legs. The valley, draped in a black shroud of soot, seemed to him like a vision from the underworld, a scene from a nightmare.

The road, a pale-yellow snake through the hills, passed between an old churchyard and a tavern. A large group of riders appeared on the road, stirring gray dust into swirling eddies. Rudyi rose slightly in his saddle, shielding his eyes with a broad hand as he tried to make out the figures.

"Are they Poles?!" Petro whispered breathlessly.

"Unlikely," Rudyi replied. "Poles wouldn't burn churches."

"Then who? The Tatars?!" Petro pressed.

"Most likely…" Rudyi murmured.

He fell silent, noticing something unusual. At the rear of the group, a rider dragged something behind him on a rope. Through the dust, it was hard to discern what it was, but even Petro guessed:

"A prisoner…"

"If they needed a prisoner, they wouldn't be dragging him like a sack," Rudyi replied, his face turning into a mask of stone. Only his eyes betrayed a fiery resolve.

"What will we do?" Petro asked, overwhelmed by helplessness. His mind spun with grim thoughts about his parents' fate.

Rudyi dismounted and handed the reins to Petro.

"Your task is to hide in that thicket and wait for me. They're unlikely to head there."

"And you?!" Petro asked anxiously. "Are you going to call for help?"

"The poor soul being dragged by that cursed janissary may still be alive," Rudyi said quietly. He checked his pistol, thrust it into Petro's belt, and disappeared into the bushes, leaving the boy alone with his fears.

Petro sank onto a fallen log, his legs numb. The pistol fell to the ground, its weight too much for his loosely tied belt. Petro picked up the heavy weapon. The silence deepened. Once, in secret from his mother, father had taught him to load a pistol and explained how to use it. Petro had even been lucky enough to fire it once or twice at wild ducks in the marshes, but to kill a man...

Nearby, the sound of hooves broke the silence. Someone shouted a foreign word so sharply it nearly knocked the young man's heart from his chest. Rudyi's horse stood calmly, only flicking an ear at the voices echoing nearby. But Petro's mare looked terrified, constantly tugging at the reins and tossing her head. The boy gently stroked her and whispered prayers to the Holy Trinity, begging that the enemy might suspect nothing.

As the strangers drew closer, the ill-fated mare reared up, neighed, snapped the branch to which she had been tied, and bolted toward the forest. One of the strangers immediately turned in the direction where Petro crouched beneath the Cossack horse, clutching the loaded pistol in his trembling, sweat-drenched hands. He tensed his index finger on the trigger so hard he could barely feel it. His thoughts fixed only on firing the moment a Janissary cap appeared above the weeds.

There was a rustling in the bushes. Petro could already hear the breathing and the pungent stench of a sweaty body overpowering even the strong scent of wormwood.

Suddenly, a guttural shout called the Tatar back. He stopped. Through the wild thudding of his pulse in his temples, Petro heard the heavy steps retreating through the tall grass. From the direction of what must already have been a dead village came the sound of howling mixed with the acrid breath of burning wood.

Hadji Bey was famed as one of the greatest warriors of Islam Giray himself. He had led many successful campaigns and displayed personal courage and loyalty to Khan during palace uprisings.

Hadji Bey was a skilled horseman and a knowledgeable commander. So, many of Gerai's enemies wanted to win him over. They tempted him with fabulous riches and promises to make him the leader of the Khan's army. Once, a high-ranking nobleman, a secret enemy of the Khan, offered Hadji Bey a divine, untouched blonde concubine from the north. She was to be the payment for crucial information.

Hadji Bey agreed. But he wanted the concubine first. Then he would give them what they wanted. Upon the slave's arrival at his harem, Hadji Bey confirmed her beauty. He then ordered the capture of the influential conspirator. The cunning warrior convinced Khan of his guilt. So, he executed the man who had given him such a valuable gift.

Such loyalty and cleverness caught Khan's attention. He drew Hadji Bey closer and began to trust him with important, secret tasks. In the Hetmanate's heart, Hadji and his best warriors were to find the agreements between the Cossacks and the Poles. A top Cossack scout had been sent on a secret mission. He was to negotiate with a Polish noble. Capturing him and extracting every piece of information he knew was a matter of honor for every warrior, especially the Khan's best.

Yet from the outset, things seemed to go awry. Hadji Bey's dog howled during the evening prayer. Its muzzle was raised to the north. It was merely a bad omen, of course, but why would such an intelligent dog, who never made a sound without permission or urgency, bark during the prayer?

The next evening, as the squad passed Perekop, a trap caught Hadji Bey's lieutenant's horse. This was an ill omen. That night, two of his best Janissaries were found decapitated. Their heads were seemingly gnawed off by some beast. The heads were left in a linen sack at his tent's entrance. Yesterday, they were ordered to visit a nearby settlement. They had to replenish food supplies at the local tavern. Also, they needed to check for any suspicious Cossacks. Gold had even been given to pay for everything, to avoid the usual bloody carnage, yet here they were, dead. Hadji Bey was furious and swore to Allah that he would turn that village into a true Christian hell.

Since the guards, even under torture, couldn't explain how the sack had ended up near the tent, they were executed to serve as a lesson to others.

Finally, this morning, the goal of the long journey was within reach. Thanks to secret informants, Hadji Bey knew precisely when and where the Cossack scheduled to meet the Polish emissary would pass. It was after that meeting that the man needed to be captured and interrogated. Cossacks were skilled warriors, but none had ever died in Hadji Bey's hands without revealing everything they knew—and even things they didn't.

Yet the ominous premonitions, fueled by sinister omens, began to come true. Old Michael, a Jewish elder and the last person to see the secret envoy from the Cossacks, was found dead. It was Hadji Bey himself who discovered him hanging in his own house. At first glance, it seemed that the elderly, lonely man had taken his own life, but the seasoned warrior did not believe in such an inconvenient coincidence.

None of the neighbors, not even under torture, could—or would—say which Cossack had visited Michael the day before.

No matter how many houses Hadji Bey burned, how many heads he severed, how many stomachs he slashed open, or how many children he impaled on spears, it was all in vain. And it infuriated him endlessly. Staying too long in the devastated village was not an option, as a Cossack patrol could appear at any moment. Yet capturing a Cossack was imperative. Islam Gerai was not only a generous and just Khan but also mercilessly brutal toward his enemies and failures.

Hadji Bey was preparing to leave the village. His men searched for the scout. A mutilated, tortured old woman told him about an armless Cossack living on the edge of the settlement. Surely, such a man would know everything.

They caught old Sobol near the forest as he was trying to flee with his wife and meager possessions. They say the devil fought fiercely, swinging his saber. He sent two Janissaries to Allah and wounded three others before they finally subdued him and dragged him to Hadji Bey.

It seemed as if his curses could be heard all the way back at the Sich. The battered lips of the stubborn warrior unleashed an endless torrent of profanity. The old Cossack swore with such fervor and such confidence in the power of his words that even the seasoned Janissaries felt chills down their spines. Eventually, they shoved a gag into the prisoner's mouth.

He fell silent, but seeing the defiant glare in his bulging eyes, Hadji Bey realized the man would not speak, even if his skin were flayed. Of course, that could be arranged, but who knew? Perhaps the Sich really had heard those frenzied curses. The scout couldn't have gotten far, so there was no time to waste.

They bound old Sobol's legs with his own belt, tied him to a saddle by his one remaining arm, and dragged him along the road. In the sweltering midday heat, a cloud of dust rose, mingling above the riders with the black smoke of burning fires.

Hadji Bey rode along the road, shielding his face from the omnipresent dust. All he wanted now was to hear from his men that the scout had been found and that they could return home. But one by one, the scouts came back empty-handed.

As they approached the forest, the riders were met with a piercing wolf's howl.

"Why do wolves howl in broad daylight?" One of Hadji Bey's lieutenants rode up to him, his two companions glancing around warily.

"Maybe one or two caught the scent of human blood," Hadji Bey replied, trying to sound indifferent. "What's this, are you more afraid of wolves than of the Cossack sharpshooters?" The man said nothing, falling back to ride alongside his comrades.

The Janissaries were brave warriors when it came to facing a tangible enemy, but tales of Cossacks with extraordinary powers often drained their fighting spirit. They would secretly share eerie stories about the "servants of Shaytan" when commanders weren't listening.

As they drew closer to the dark-green mass of the forest, the wolves' howls grew louder. It was clear that more than just one or two predators were howling. Somewhere nearby, a large pack had gathered.

Hadji Bey glanced at his subordinates and yanked on the rope tied to the prisoner. The captive groaned hoarsely, his swollen, bruised hand clenching into a fist. "What are you standing around for?" the Tatar snapped at the riders. "Get moving and find that scout, or I'll flay the skin off you instead of him!"

He lashed his horse with a whip and galloped toward the forest, kicking up a cloud of dust. On one side of the beaten track stood towering oaks; on the other was a steep slope. Somewhere nearby, Hadji Bey was supposed to rendezvous with two of his scouts.

In the sweltering heat, even the leaves on the trees seemed to have frozen in anticipation. The Janissary halted his horse. The road curved ahead, disappearing into the forest. There was no sign of his men behind him. Hadji Bey was alone.

He dismounted, adjusted his robe, and slowly approached the lifeless Sobol. The prisoner was no longer breathing. With one swift motion, the Tatar leader cut the rope, spat on the contorted body of the captive, and suddenly heard a low, menacing growl nearby.

Rudyi lay hidden on the roadside of the deserted path. Along with the smoke from the burnt-out ruins, a faint breeze carried the sound of voices and hoofbeats drawing closer. As soon as Ivan saw the rider dragging the mutilated body of old Sobol behind him, he recognized the man immediately. It was one of the few Tatars faces he would never forget.

Rudyi first encountered Hadji Bey many years ago, when he was captured during one of his scouting missions beyond Perekop. Trapped in a dark dungeon alongside his comrades, the young Cossack thought he was already dead. It was easier to accept the end than to hope that someone might remember him and pay the ransom. The only thing that troubled Ivan at the time was how he would be executed. He wasn't sure he could endure the torture with dignity. But days of waiting proved far worse than the cruelest death. So, when Rudyi and the others were led into a wide courtyard, he welcomed it as long-awaited relief from the humiliating captivity and his own fears.

A third of the yard was taken up by an enclosure where enormous wolves paced impatiently. It was Ivan's first time seeing live adult wolves so close.

Hadji Bey moved slowly from one prisoner to the next, locking eyes with each of them, savoring the terror hidden within. Then he would signal the Janissaries to toss the Cossack into the enclosure. The wolves, likely starved for days, tore the victims apart in mere minutes. Rudyi could still hear the screams of those poor souls years later.

Finally, it was his turn. The Tatar scrutinized his face, his young, muscular body, as though he were inspecting goods at a market.

"The wolves are nearly full," he finally said, "so they'll take their time eating you."

Ivan gritted his teeth and said nothing.

"You're young and strong," Hadji Bey continued, "I think I could make you a worthy warrior of Allah."

Ivan raised his eyes to the Tatar.

"When I get out of there, I'll tear your throat out myself."

Hadji Bey froze for a moment, weighing whether to slaughter the insolent man on the spot or to let the bloody spectacle continue.

"My father fought with Hetman Khmelnytsky against the Polish king," he said calmly. "He believed Cossacks were good warriors but too foolish to use their strength."

"We didn't ask a stinking Tatar how to live our lives..."

"To the wolves with him!" Hadji Bey screeched.

Rudyi didn't remember how long he spent in that enclosure. He sat on the blood-soaked sand and rested his head on his knees. He imagined himself as one of the wolves. Their wet noses sniffed at him from all sides. This exercise, taught to him by Otaman Sirko, helped him fend off the fear of death, whose breath he felt on him every moment. But death's scythe didn't touch his soul that day, perhaps busy with other matters.

Half-conscious from thirst, he was dragged out of the enclosure by disappointed Janissaries. Later, Rudyi learned that it was Ivan Sirko himself who paid gold for his release.

And now, here was that same Tatar, just steps away, alone, dragging Sobol's body behind him. Ivan reached for his saber. But... there would never be a better moment to fulfill the promise he had once made. Tilting his head toward the scorching sky, the mystic howled like a wolf.

"Are you sure he took this road?" one Janissary asked another. The other nodded.

"How could you leave your commander alone?" "He was in too much of a hurry after that stinking goat herder..."

The unit rode out onto the empty road. Near the roadside lay a bloodied body.

"He must've left him and gone on to find the scout," one of the warriors suggested.

As they approached, the Janissaries saw that the body lying on the road was Hadji Bey's. His head, torn off by sharp fangs, lay in the dust nearby. There was no sign of his horse or the one-armed prisoner. Only the tracks of wolf paws circled the area.

Chapter Six

Until this moment, Petro had never seen a tortured corpse. His father lay in a hastily dug grave. Despite his body being a mass of wounds, he looked almost alive, his face bearing the same expression Petro had seen every day. There was nothing about him that suggested death. It seemed to lurk, hidden behind closed eyelids. Father was indistinguishable from that of living. Petro half expected his father to open his eyes at any moment and look at him with his usual mix of jest and sternness.

The boy stood frozen over the open grave, unable to look away. A slow nausea rose in his throat. It was fueled by a despair and anguish far more intense than anything he'd felt when he heard about his brother's death. These emotions swelled, desperate to escape as either a scream or vomit. Only the presence of Uncle Rudyi kept Petro standing rigid over his father, like a stone idol.

Rudyi gently took the crooked shovel handle from young Sobol. The boy's hands trembled. Then, Rudyi began throwing damp soil into the grave. The heavy clumps of earth landed on the body and scattered into smaller pieces.

Only the single arm and head of old Sobol remained uncovered. Suddenly, the lifeless hand rose, shaking off the dirt, and the eyes snapped open. But they weren't his father's, they were his brother's. The sight knocked Petro back from the grave, a chill coursing through him, and then... he awoke.

The stars on the dark mourning cloth of the night sky twinkled in chaotic splendor, as if apologizing for the terror they had brought him. Petro tried to steady his breath. The steppe sang a sad ballad. Mosquitoes buzzed over his sweaty forehead. He slapped his cheek, leaving a dark stain on his palm.

"Drunken pests," he thought. It was likely his first coherent thought. His throat was parched, his tongue sticking to the roof of his mouth. Petro stood up. As far as the eye could see, the steppe stretched endlessly beneath the transparent night sky. In the east, the horizon began to blush faintly, heralding the approaching dawn.

Remembering his dream, Petro shivered. A sudden thought struck him—if it weren't for that peculiar Cossack, his parents might still be alive. It was Rudyi who had brought death to his family. As unrelenting grief churned in his chest, it gave birth to burning anger and an overwhelming urge to act immediately. Even if devils from hell aided this *kharakternyk*, Petro would not be deterred. His body trembled, not from cold or fear, but from the pain that urged him to act. His hand found the knife hidden in his boot as he silently stood.

Rudyi sat nearby, cross-legged, in the center of a circle of trampled grass. When Petro called him, he didn't stir. Bathed in pale moonlight, the Cossack resembled a lone stone figure in the vast emptiness of the wild steppe. Steeling himself, Petro moved closer and realized Rudyi was entirely naked. Wooden stakes of equal length protruded from the ground, their ends tied with strips of fabric, forming a square. The steppe wind played with the cloth like a child clapping hand. Creeping closer, Petro strained to understand the peculiar sight. Amid the monotone whispers of the steppe, he began to hear a hum-like chant. It was Rudyi—whether he was singing or howling with the night wind, Petro couldn't tell.

A twig cracked under Petro's foot. Rudyi turned his head, and Petro nearly screamed. The Cossack's pale face and blazing enlarged eyes radiated an unearthly terror that froze the boy in place. The knife slipped from his hands.

"Uncle Rudyi, is that you?" Petro wanted to ask, but his lips refused to move. His tongue felt like dry sawdust, glued to his throat. Then someone pushed him from behind. Petro turned his stiff body and saw... Rudyi.

The harsh sunlight beat down on his face as Rudyi shook him awake. The deep wrinkles on the Cossack's forehead betrayed worry. "Enough sleeping," Rudyi said as Petro blinked groggily, trying to grasp reality. "The Tatars will have you on a stake, and you wouldn't even notice."

Petro sat up, shaking his head.

"I had such a dream..." he muttered, rubbing his eyes. "You scared me, Uncle. May the devil take you!"

Suddenly, Petro remembered his intent to kill Rudyi. Whether it had truly happened or was just a nightmare, he wasn't sure. Embarrassment flooded him with the thought that Rudyi might have guessed his mad impulse. What had come over him?

"Get up!" Rudyi ordered. "Keep sleeping, and you'll scare yourself even more." The Cossack stood, scanned the horizon with sharp eyes, and adjusted his saber. His focused and combative demeanor snapped Petro out of his daze, and he jumped to his feet.

"What's happening? Are the Tatars close?"

"Three or four riders," Rudyi said confidently. "They'll appear from the southeast any moment now."

Petro stared at him in amazement.

"Did you see them?"

"Hmm... you could say that," Rudyi replied, a cryptic smile hidden beneath his long mustache.

Petro's eyes widened in surprise.

"How did you manage to scout so quickly? The horizon is clear!" "Too much knowledge will pop your eyes out," Rudyi quipped. "We need to find cover."

Petro glanced around skeptically.

"Where would we hide? It's just open steppe..."

His gaze dropped to Rudyi's broad shoulder and then to the stakes tied with cloth behind him. A chill ran down Petro's spine, and he instinctively stepped back.

"Uncle Ivan," he said, barely moving his tongue, "what is this for?" "Do as I say and stop questioning everything," Rudyi snapped. "Then, maybe, you'll live. Our guests are coming."

The Cossack gestured toward the horizon, where the faint outline of a dust cloud was now visible. At first, Petro saw nothing, but as he squinted, he noticed it too. Moments earlier, the horizon had been clear. Panic surged as he realized there was nowhere to hide—no trees, no bushes, not even a ditch. Running seemed futile. But why wasn't Rudyi in a hurry?

Petro dared not voice his thoughts as Rudyi's expression changed. His face darkened, his features sharp with focus. He looked like a wild beast ready to strike. Was he planning to fight?

"Get in the circle," Rudyi commanded in a low, steady voice.

Petro hesitated but obeyed, sitting in the grass within the marked area. He watched the dust cloud grow closer, bringing with it the specter of death. The boy couldn't decide what frightened him more—the approaching Tatar riders or the strange Cossack, who seemed half-mad or perhaps truly a *kharakternyk*. When Petro had heard tales about them, he'd longed to see one in person. Now, all he wanted was to flee. But how could he escape from Tatars—or a *kharakternyk*?

Meanwhile, Rudyi ignored Petro entirely, as if the Tatars didn't exist. He busied himself with strange tasks: positioning the horses—Petro's mare and his own—tail-to-tail within the circle. He whispered something into each horse's ear as Petro gawked, mouth agape.

When Rudyi finished, he sat beside Petro, drew his saber, and thrust it deep into the ground, up to the hilt.

"How will he draw it now?" Petro wondered silently.

The sound of hoofbeats and guttural shouts grew louder. Petro squeezed his eyes shut, bracing for the cold steel of a blade on his neck. Maybe Rudyi would delay death, but only briefly.

Minutes passed. The voices shouted, horses snorted, and then... nothing.

Petro cracked his eyes open and saw six Tatar riders circling near Rudyi's staked formation. They examined the area, arguing among themselves. They ignored the two horses and the figures sitting in the circle.

Chapter Seven

The Sich sometimes resembled a cauldron over a roaring fire, filled with a rich and enticing stew for any free-spirited soul. Life bubbled within it with passion. Its vibrant essence rose skyward. The air was full of smoke from campfires and hearths. It was filled with the clang of sabers, boisterous laughter, jokes, curses, and echoes of Cossack councils.

Rudyi and Petro entered on foot through the gates; the boy's mare had not survived the journey. Rudyi's horse trudged alongside them, dignified yet weary. Petro struggled to stay upright, but his exhaustion transformed into curiosity. He gazed at the inhabitants of the Sich as though they were celestial beings.

These "angels" roamed the dusty, wide streets between low, elongated barracks. They wore leather trousers or Rudyi's broad Turkish silk ones. Their shirts were greasy and sometimes bloodstained. Sabers nestled in their armpits, while pairs of pistols jutted from leather belts.

Many bored arms or legs are bandaged. Three such figures suddenly rushed at Rudyi, embracing him and playfully hurling curses. To

Petro's amazement, Rudyi did not push away these drunken louts. Instead, his previously stern face lit up with a broad, toothy smile, and he rushed to meet them. They embraced, slapping each other on the back.

"Where have those damned Tatars been dragging you, you barrel-bellied devil?" Petro had never seen Rudyi so cheerful. He had always spoken calmly, almost to himself, but now he was a different man.

"They dragged me but couldn't wear me down, brother!" Rudyi boomed in reply, slapping his chest with his large, calloused hands. "No cursed infidel could ever conquer a true Cossack spirit!"

Suddenly, the man grew serious and spoke quietly:

"We know you did more than anyone to free us from captivity. For that, we owe you our lives. Thank you."

All three solemnly bowed to Rudyi.

A massive hand landed on Petro's shoulder.

"Rudyi, I see you've already found yourself a page," a deep voice rumbled from above his head. "Can't carry your saber on your own anymore?"

Rudyi turned toward the voice.

"This is Sobol's younger son," he said evenly. "He'll stay with me for now. If he agrees, he'll be a proper Cossack in a year or two."

Petro's face burned with sudden heat.

A tall Cossack in a vibrant blue coat emerged from behind Petro, placed his hands on his hips, and began scrutinizing the boy. His deeply set eyes peered so intently that it seemed as though he was trying to glimpse Petro's very soul. At that moment, Petro was certain the man had succeeded.

"So, Sobol dared to send his youngest to the Sich?" the man asked. "He wouldn't have dared, Ataman, had death not claimed him by a Tatar's hand," Rudyi replied quietly.

The Ataman shook his head. "Death is a stranger's bride, isn't it?" he said softly.

Petro felt as though these words were meant to console him. After all, he hadn't yet fully grasped that he was now utterly alone in the world—without a father, a mother, or a brother.

"Let's head to the barracks. We have matters to discuss," the tall Cossack said to Rudyi. "Let your page spend some time with the brothers. They'll show him what the Sich is all about."

The barrack they entered was built from finely hewn logs, towering over the others. It was noticeably larger and taller. Crossing himself and bowing to the icon, Rudyi took a seat on a bench. The spacious room was cool and empty. Sirko settled in the corner, adjusted himself, and cast a piercing gaze at Rudyi.

"What news do you bring from the north?" Sirko asked curtly. "The Poles are asking for help against the Tatars," Rudyi replied. "When they ask for something, it always means trouble," Sirko muttered, almost to himself.

pulled a sack of gold from his bag and placed it on the is their reward?" the Ataman asked. "They promise more if we take the Tatar fortress we discussed earlier." "They promise... Do they truly think they can pay for my men's lives with cursed gold? How much longer will the Sich serve as the Polish king's shield against the Tatars?"

Rudyi remained silent, his eyes cast down. Only the tension in his jaw betrayed his suppressed anger. He remembered every man who had fallen in battles for foreign interests. Their faces haunted him nightly when he could no longer bear the sight of the world.

"We do have our interests in this matter," Rudyi said quietly.

Sirko shook his head, twisting his long, dyed mustache. He rose heavily from his corner and retrieved a large bottle, two cups, and a small pot with wooden dishes and spoons.

"The potaptsi[11] are cold," the Ataman said apologetically as he poured them drinks. "They make it just for me here."

Rudyi waved it off, feeling somewhat awkward at Sirko's warm hospitality, and quickly downed his drink. The mead dripped down his mustache, but Rudyi swiftly caught the drops with his sleeve and began eating. Sirko did the same.

"I called you, Ivan, for another reason," Sirko said, setting down his cup. "The Poles can wait."

Rudyi looked up at the Ataman.

---

[11] Potaptsi — sort of Ukrainian tradition food.

"I know you're eager for that fortress," Sirko continued, "because you left your heart within those walls. But right now, I need your help, and you're the only one I can turn to."

Sirko smirked at his words. He was the Ataman of the famed Zaporizhian Host, yet there was only one man he could rely on.

"There's something we need—not just for me, but for the benefit of the entire Sich," he said.

"And what might that be?" Rudyi asked.

"A mace, but not an ordinary one," Sirko replied, leaning toward his comrade. His voice dropped to a whisper, but Rudyi heard every word.

"It's said the Volhvs who lived along the left bank of the Dnipro over a thousand years ago forged it. The mace holds great power if you know how to unlock it."

"Where is this mace now?"

Sirko explained its journey. It had passed through a Polish nobleman, ruined his family, and ended up in the Tatar Khan's treasury.

Sirko filled their cups again and drank deeply before growling into his sleeve.

"I wanted to retrieve it myself," he said hoarsely, "but constant disputes on the Sich have kept me here. So, I'm asking you, Ivan—steal that mace from the infidels for me."

Rudyi smiled faintly and slammed his cup against the oak table.

"stolen enough from under the Tatars' noses before?" he

Sirko raised a cautionary hand.

"This is different," he said gravely. "I'm almost certain they know what they've got, and they'll guard it well."

For another half hour, the two Cossacks discussed their plans in hushed tones. As they prepared to part, Rudyi turned to Sirko: "Look after young Sobol here. I hope he'll make a fine Cossack—if he doesn't falter."

"You can count on me," Sirko replied. "I owe his brother, as you know…"

Chapter Eight

Why was it so cold today? This was the only question murza Davlet-bey asked himself as he listened to the echo of hoofbeats against the cobblestones. He rode alone, without guards. The Khan himself required it. The city slept, blanketed in dense, milky fog.

It was so early that not even the dogs barked at the lone rider. The muezzin would not call for morning prayer for at least another hour. There wasn't a single soul in sight. Beneath the somber sky, the color of a burial shroud, Davlet-bey felt a creeping unease. He was on his way to meet an unknown imam from Istanbul.

The murza had received a secret letter about the imam's arrival several weeks earlier. He could not understand why the infidels' newly found mace was so important to Islam Giray. They obtained it under mysterious circumstances. The Khan had spared no expense in inviting a Turkish imam.

The question had kept Davlet-bey awake through the night and still gnawed at him now. The Tatar sensed a hidden mystery behind it and was determined to uncover the truth at any cost.

A quarter remained before reaching the city gates. They went into a street lined with caravanserais. Here, the fog lightened slightly. From time to time, ghostly figures emerged from the shadows onto the road, bowing deeply to the rider before vanishing again. Looming ahead in the mist, the dark towers of the gates rose sharply into view. The distant voices of unseen guards brought a small measure of comfort.

Suddenly, a door creaked open nearby. A man darted out, wearing a gaudy and dirty robe, with a disheveled turban perched at an angle on his head. Without hesitation, he grabbed the murza's horse by the reins and bowed so low that his turban nearly brushed the cobblestones.

Davlet-bey nearly choked on his fury. For a moment, he couldn't decide whether to strike the insolent man with his whip or simply curse him. But then his eyes caught the hilt of a saber hidden beneath the folds of the man's robe. The stranger's gaze was sharp and spiteful, unlike any innkeeper's. His brows were furrowed.

"Do not spurn my hospitality, honorable murza," rasped the man, his voice as unpleasant as his appearance. No common caravanserai keeper could possess such a voice—or such a piercing glare.

Davlet-bey dismounted slowly, striving to appear composed and superior.

The strange host tossed the reins to a servant. He bowed repeatedly to the ground and, with a broad, calloused hand, gestured for the murza to follow. Even in the dim morning light, Davlet-bey couldn't help but notice the man's rough, muscular palm—more suited to wielding a sword than counting coins.

Inside, the air was damp and dark. The caravanserai was not merely modest; it bordered on being a refuge for beggars. The thought crossed the murza's mind: if this imam were truly a respected guest invited by the Khan himself, why would he choose such a wretched place to rest? Or had Davlet-bey walked into a trap set by common thieves? Yet retreat was no longer an option. The sharp, needle-like eyes of his guide never left him. The only solace lay in the fact that Davlet-bey carried little of value beyond his clothes. His primary goal now was to escape alive and unharmed.

They climbed a shadowy staircase to the second floor. Silently obeying the guide's abrupt gestures, Davlet-bey stepped into a small room. A curtain concealed one corner. Seated cross-legged on the floor was a man dressed in the rags of a beggar. The oily light of a lamp cast a yellow glow over his slender figure and pale face, giving him the appearance of a phantom.

Davlet-bey's heart sank—there was no doubt this was a member of the tasawwuf[12]: a secret Sufi order of powerful mystics. Indifferent to wealth or power, their magical prowess and wisdom were the stuff of legend.

"Did the esteemed murza follow the Khan's command to arrive without guards?" asked the man in a voice as hollow as the grave.

Davlet-bey nodded silently.

---

[12] in Arabic, tasawwuf, is an umbrella term which refers to the inner mystical dimension of Islam. The same linguistic root also generates from the word for wool in Arabic; hence, a Sufi is one who wears a wool, or suf, garment.

"Even hidden watchers could disrupt the plans of the noble Khan," the mystic's voice resonated with an eerie echo.

"I followed my master's orders to the letter," Davlet-bey replied, "and I am fully prepared to assist in any way with this secret mission entrusted to me."

The glowing eyes of the tasawwuf, like those of a ghoul, fixed on the murza.

"Yes, I hope you will serve your Khan well," the strange beggar said, his tone heavy with unspoken warnings. "But know this—I will see every thought and intention that crosses your mind. You cannot deceive me. Do only what you are told."

The murza bowed his head obediently.

"I am ready to carry out my orders at once if this is my master's will," he declared.

"Take my envoy to the place where the Khan keeps the mace. Arrange lodging for him nearby, but do not set guards. Ensure that not even your servants know of your actions. Be cautious, for the enemy has already sent spies into this esteemed city.

Davlet-bey remained bowing, relieved. This assignment presented a rare opportunity to win favor with the Khan. It was futile to learn more about the mysterious mace from this cunning tasawwuf. But, the murza knew his methods for getting the info he needed.

"My envoy will wait by the mosque in two hours when the sun rises above the city gate," the mystic continued. "You have enough time to make the necessary arrangements."

"Yes, master," Davlet-bey replied. "Are there any other instructions regarding this mission?"

The beggar waved his hand, signaling that the meeting was over.

As Davlet-bey turned toward the door, the tasawwuf's quiet voice reached him again.

"One more piece of advice..."

"I am listening, master."

"I see your heart as an open scroll in a brilliant light. If you poke your nose where it doesn't belong, I promise you will regret it.

When the heavy door closed, the curtain stirred and drew back as if moved by an unseen hand. A woman, adorned in opulent eastern garments, appeared before the tasawwuf. She knelt at his feet and kissed the hem of his tattered robe.

"I am ready to fulfill your every wish, my master," she whispered.

The mystic shifted his gaze from the door to the bowed head of his concubine. His eyes softened.

"But you are afraid," he said. "Did I not teach you to fear nothing?"

"I fear not my enemies, master," the woman replied. "And I am unafraid to give my life in battle. But a strange foreboding has taken root in my chest."

"Tell me of it," the mystic said, his voice filled with patience and tenderness, as though a father were speaking to his daughter.

"My life feels as though it is on the verge of splitting in two, and my heart will shatter from the unbearable sorrow and pain," she said. "Yet let my master not be angered by his servant for burdening his great mind. I will carry out my duties even at the cost of my soul. But you commanded me to share every movement of my heart. I only obey your orders."

The broad, calloused hand of her teacher rested lightly on her head. "You have done well," he said gently. "I see your soul suffers, and there is nothing in this world that can ease its torment. But remember this is because of that suffering that you are now a renowned warrior of Allah. May His name be praised!"

Though his hand never pressed upon her head, the woman sank even lower to the ground, as if an invisible weight had descended upon her shoulders.

Chapter nine

Has anyone ever written in thick, time-yellowed scrolls about how a person transforms into a wolf? What do they feel at that moment? Do any of those bookworms know what it's like to exist as a beast while retaining a human soul? Only the kharakternyks, men like Ivan Rudyi, know the truth of such an existence.

Nonsense abounds about them. Their enemies fear even the thought of a kharakternyk. He is nearly impossible to kill. No one can match him in war. He can see into his opponent's soul and predict their moves. Who today could be a worthy adversary in battle against such a warrior-seer? If such a rival exists, Rudyi has yet to hear of them.

Indeed, few kharakternyks remain; their power is fading into the past. But as long as they endure, the Sich will stand firm...

These thoughts came to Ivan not out of pride in his abilities but from the weight of the night's mission. He was to infiltrate a fortified Tatar city. There, he must steal a magical mace, as Sirko had said. Then, he must return alive and unscathed. Yet he would not do it for the mace itself or for the glory of Cossack victories. After all, a Cossack can hold his ground without otherworldly sorcery. No, he would do it because of a promise to old Sobol about his youngest son, Petro. A dying, one-armed Cossack on that forest road, littered with Tatar bodies, had wrenched that vow from Rudyi's soul. It was perhaps the only moment in human history where man and beast so perfectly understood one another without speaking a single word.

Thus, Rudyi had to return alive and teach the boy everything he needed to know—not necessarily as a kharakternyk, but as a good Cossack.

The night was deep, and the fire had long since turned to ash. The sky, adorned with the Milky Way's necklace of stars, was as clear as a woodland pond and seemed so close, like a delicate silk sheet draped over the earth.

As the wind played among the wild steppe grasses, Ivan Rudyi drifted into sleep.

He was born and raised in a free Cossack settlement in a family of a regimental scribe in Poltava. A fine young lad, he loved hard work and, from almost childhood, wielded a saber with great skill. His uncle, who visited once or twice a year from the Sich, had taught him the cunning art of swordsmanship.

When his uncle arrived, he would gather the village children near the root cellar. Then, he would tell fantastic tales. He fought the Turks, reached Constantinople, and defeated the Poles. Khmel[13] had once sent him on a dangerous mission near Przemysl, where he had turned into a wolf to terrify the enemy.

---

[13] Hetman Bogran Khmelnytsky

No one knew if the stories were true or made up. After Ivan's mother chased the young listeners home with a broom, he would lie awake for hours, pondering: what does it feel like when a man becomes a wolf?

There were rumors in the village that old Yavdokha, the herbalist, could turn into a black cat and cross the paths of good people. But she was just an old crone, and there was a Cossack...

Ivan first met Yarina when the older boys took him caroling to a neighboring village. He had just turned thirteen, and it was the first time his parents had let him go so far.

Though many years had passed, Rudyii remembered their first encounter vividly. A small, slender girl in a neat dress ran out to greet the guests, her warm smile and cheerful voice like a bell. She couldn't have been more than ten.

The first thing Ivan did was hide behind his older friend's back. But Yarina's open, joyous gaze quickly dissolved his shyness. Stepping forward to greeting her, Ivan slipped and fell face-first into the snow at her feet. The laughter that erupted from the village that night was something it would long remember.

Yarina would occasionally visit Ivan's village with her mother. Ivan often ran ten versts to see her, sneaking away from home, for which he was invariably scolded.

As Ivan grew into a striking young man, his wealthy parents were cautious about Yarina. She lived with only her mother and had no dowry.

"There are plenty of girls around, and you've chosen the poorest one," his father would grumble whenever the topic of marriage arose.

"I have hands, and God hasn't deprived me of sense. I'll earn everything myself," Ivan would reply, and the conversation would end there.

Everything changed when rumors spread of Polish cavalry nearby. They said the Poles had burned Baturyn[14] and were ravaging every village in their path on their way back.

"Thank God we're not on their road," Ivan's mother said, crossing herself before an icon.

"But they might be tempted by the village where Yarina lives," Ivan replied, leaping to his feet.

"Son don't go there, for Christ's sake," his mother pleaded, but Ivan didn't listen.

"Don't take the horse out in this blizzard!" came his father's voice.

Hearing the doors slam in the entryway, his mother turned to the icon and began praying. His father sat silently at the table, staring at the frost-painted window and twisting his long mustache...

Ivan ran until he couldn't breathe anymore. He stopped, his chest heaving, and looked around. He was in the winter forest. Silence

---

[14] Baturyn (Ukrainian: Батурин) is a historic city of northern Ukraine. It is located in Nizhyn district on the banks of the Seym River. In 1648 Baturyn was transformed into a Cossack regional center (sotnia) ↑

enveloped him, broken only by the creak of snow underfoot. Could he be lost? No, that wasn't possible, he knew the path to Yaryna's little house at the edge of the village as well as knowing his own hand, even blindfolded. But now, everything was obscured by deep snowdrifts.

Ivan turned around. The trees around him were black against the blinding white. Their snow-laden branches resembled mourners draped in funeral shrouds. They looked like cracks leading into another world.

A sudden chill ran down his spine, but Ivan quickly regained his bearings. If he could just reach that clearing, the forest would end. Then there would be a small frozen pond, and beyond it, the village. From the pond's far shore, he'd see Yaryna's house perched on its hilltop—a familiar beacon.

He and Yaryna had often met here on summer evenings, counting stars in the vast, clear sky.

When Ivan reached the clearing, his breath caught. Yaryna stood in the middle of the frozen pond, dressed only in a thin shift, her hair loose and wild. She stared at him and seemed to be speaking, but he couldn't hear her words. Her lips, blue from the cold, moved, forming a phrase he couldn't decipher.

"Yaryna!" Ivan shouted. Sliding down the snow-covered hill, he ran onto the ice. It cracked and groaned under his weight, splintering into dark veins. Black, viscous water oozed from the cracks, clawing at his boots, threatening to swallow him whole.

He was only five or six steps away from her when the ice beneath Yaryna shattered with a sharp, echoing crack. She let out a piercing scream as she plunged into the frigid depths. Ivan watched, horrified, as her head surfaced amid the freezing water, her hair plastered to her face, her wide eyes locked on his.

"Hold on!" Ivan shouted, dropping to his stomach and crawling forward. He reached out and grasped her icy hand.

"I'll pull you out!" he cried, his voice trembling with desperation.

Yaryna looked at him, and her voice remained steady and serene despite the chaos around them. "You shouldn't have come to save me, Ivan," she said. "You'll find your death here..."

The words struck him like a thunderclap. He realized she had been repeating this phrase since the moment he'd first seen her in the clearing. He had not been able to hear it at all.

Yaryna's head dipped below the surface, and with a sudden, unrelenting force, she pulled Ivan downward. He fought back with all his strength, clutching the ice shards. But, the freezing water dragged him deeper, wrapping around him like a shroud.

Ivan woke with a start, his heart racing. The steppe stretched endlessly around him, bathed in the cold light of dawn. The sky to the east was beginning to brighten.

Yaryna rarely visited him in dreams, but this one had been so vivid it left a bitter ache in his chest. When he arrived at her burned-out home all those years ago, he found only the body of her frail mother. The neighbors had conflicting stories. Some said the Poles had drowned Yaryna in the lake. Others claimed they'd taken her with them.

Over a decade had passed since that day. Ivan tried not to think of her, but sometimes, when he least expected it, she came back to him.

"What a dream," he muttered, shaking his head to clear it.

The eastern sky was now streaked with hues of pink and orange, promising the arrival of a new day. Ivan stood, brushed the frost from his coat, and adjusted his weapons. The weight of the night's mission returned to him, settling like an iron chain across his shoulders.

The magical mace awaited him in the fortified city. But Ivan Rudyi, kharakternyk and Cossack, had never let fear or doubt deter him.

He cast one last glance at the fading stars overhead. "Yaryna," he whispered to the wind, "if you're watching, I'll make it back. I promise."

With that, he turned his gaze toward the horizon and strode forward into the dawning light, ready to face whatever lay ahead.

Chapter Ten

"I have always regarded the Turkish Sultan—may Allah bless him with long life—as my greatest ally, no matter what venomous tongues might say," declared Islam Giray, pacing the room with his hands clasped behind his back. His sharp eyes bore into the tasawwuf, scrutinizing him with the precision of a hawk. "But it does strike me as peculiar that instead of sending an experienced and wise imam, he has dispatched a beggar—complete with a concubine."

The tasawwuf inclined his head, not so much out of respect but to conceal the flicker of disdain in his eyes.

"I assure you," the sage replied in a steady tone, "the Sultan has sent the best suited to fulfill the task that Allah has placed before you."

The tasawwuf would not have crossed the Pontus to stand before this Tatar ruler and endure his insults. But, they sought ancient power tied to this land's mystics. Diplomacy had never been his strength, and patience for such formalities was thin. His sole hope was that the artifact—the mace—was genuine.

"If what my scholars have told me about this object is true," Islam Giray mused, "then seize its power and ensure my neighbor, the

Tatar Khan, does not harness it. If he cannot secure it without our help, then he does not deserve his fate." The Khan's words bore the edge of a command wrapped in feigned detachment, echoing the Sultan's decree.

The Khan turned away, his richly adorned robes swirling. "Perhaps so, perhaps not. These walls are rife with ears and eyes not my own. Day and night, conspirators dream of overthrowing me."

"Those ears and eyes," murmured the tasawwuf, "are less dangerous than those who covet the mace's power for themselves."

Islam Giray spun to face him, his expression dark beneath his elaborate turban. "What do you mean?"

"As I have learned, Khan," the sage began, "the mace was forged centuries ago by northern sorcerers—your people might call them volkhvs[15]. They wielded knowledge lost to most of the world, and this mace is a key to their immense power."

The Khan's eyes ignited with a fiery intensity. He strode close to the tasawwuf, radiating a restrained ferocity. The sage could feel the ruler's impulse to grab him, to shake every ounce of knowledge from him. But the Khan held back, wary of the Sultan's influence.

"And how does one wield such power?" Islam Giray asked. His voice sound sharp and probing.

---

[15] A volkhv(Cyrillic: Волхв), translatable as wiseman, wizard, sorcerer, magus) is a priest in ancient Slavic religions and contemporary Slavic Native Faith.

The tasawwuf met his gaze evenly. "To command its power, we require one who already possesses the strength to harness it."

The Khan's lips curled into a skeptical smirk. "And where might we find such a person? Surely you don't believe those tales of superhuman warriors from the Borysthenes[16]?"

"My faith is irrelevant," the sage replied. "The Sultan has tasked me with this mission, and by Allah's grace and your cooperation, Khan, I will accomplish the impossible."

The Khan held his gaze for a moment longer, then turned away. "See that you do."

With a deep bow, the tasawwuf left the sunlit hall. Islam Giray watched him until the heavy doors closed.

"If he's truly the sorcerer they say he is," the Khan muttered, "he should have sensed your presence."

From a hidden alcove at the far end of the hall, emerged a pale and trembling Davlet-Bey. He vainly tried to suck in his belly.

"I hope, my Khan, that this wretched Turk suspected nothing," he "Then he's no sorcerer, merely a fraud!" the Khan declared loudly. "The vizier's palace is riddled with secret chambers. Watch his every move and find a reason to accuse him of espionage. If he's truly the Sultan's prized emissary, he'll become a valuable pawn in our negotiations."

---

[16] In Greek mythology the Borysthenes was a river-god of Scythia in north-eastern Europe (modern Ukraine)

The murza hesitated, his face pale. "Forgive me, my lord, but perhaps this delicate matter would be better suited to someone with... more skill?"

Islam Giray closed the distance between them in a flash, fixing the murza with a piercing glare. Davlet-Bey recoiled, his head sinking into his shoulders like a cornered thief.

"I have no one else to entrust with this," the Khan growled. "Too many in this city already wish me dead. I will expose the traitors in time, but this cannot wait. You will handle it. Unless, of course, you wish to answer for your falsified debt records in the vizier's ledgers."

The murza sank to his knees. "I... I would not dare think such a thing, my lord."

In the quiet halls of the vizier's residence, the mace rested in its treasury mystical artifact sought by rulers and sages alike. Yet no one posed a greater threat than one unseen adversary, drawing closer by the hour.

The tasawwuf feared this shadowy figure far more than the Khan or his armies. Killing the intruder outright wasn't an option—the enigmatic foe was the only means to unlocking the mace's full potential. For the sage, this was the ultimate test.

Standing on the marble terrace, the tasawwuf awaited the confrontation. The city below slumbered in the embrace of midnight, its silence broken only by the sporadic cries of dogs and watchmen.

A sudden flutter of wings disturbed the stillness. A great falcon alighted on the parapet, preening its feathers with meticulous care.

"Well met, my friend," the tasawwuf said softly, studying the bird. "You know why I summoned you."

From his robes, he produced a morsel of fresh meat, which the falcon tore into eagerly. When it had finished, the sage placed a hand on its head, closing his eyes as he murmured a low chant.

"Fly!" he commanded softly but firmly, without opening his eyes. He had no need to; he saw through the keen eyes of his loyal falcon, which instantly disappeared into the night's abyss. The sage knelt, resting his hands on the cool marble floor, and became perfect still.

A faint streak of light remained. The vizier's residence, Murza Davlet-Bey's opulent mansion, and the eastern city's scattered lights had faded into the shadows.

A great, round moon suddenly pierced through a gap in the dark gray clouds, casting its pale glow over the world below. Within moments, the tasawwuf, through the falcon's sharp vision, could see everything as clearly as if it were a bright, sunny morning.

The falcon circled the city once, then veered northwest. Invisible magical threads seemed to stretch toward the one destined to wield the mace.

The wild steppe appeared barren, extending into the vast distance, to the mighty river and the first hidden posts of the Cossacks. The sage grew uneasy. The intruder was either on another path, or the tasawwuf had missed him. A skilled scout could take an alternate route.

Finally, he directed the falcon to turn back and recheck the area near the city. Beyond Perekop, the falcon spotted four campfires arranged in a small, precise quadrangle. Obediently, the bird descended closer to the ground so the tasawwuf could better observe through its eyes. But among the nearly extinguished embers, there was nothing—no people, no activity, only the free wind of the steppe. The scout, aided by magic, remained unseen, even to the falcon. Likely, he had transformed into a creature, a lynx or a wolf.

The stage opened his eyes. The corners of his thin lips curled upward, etching a web of deep wrinkles across his hollow cheeks. It was a predator's grin—the expression of a master puppeteer about to unveil a brilliant act. The tasawwuf stood, adjusting his humble turban. The trap was set. All that remained was to rouse the bait.

Mariam. That was the name he had given her when he purchased her from a suspicious trader in Ankara. Before the deal, the tasawwuf had wandered the market. Disguised as a noble murza, he examined the newly arrived slaves from northern merchants. Most were young girls or beautiful women, priced exorbitantly as fresh goods often were. Buyers scrutinized them closely, loudly haggling over prices, gesturing emphatically, and nervously tugging at their beards.

The tasawwuf had been about to leave when he was intercepted by a gaunt, elderly man in shabby attire who nearly threw himself at his feet. The man urgently offered to sell him an extraordinarily fine slave for a suspiciously low price—cheap enough to make one doubt her quality. Initially dismissing the offer as deceit, the sage paid him no mind, but the man persisted.

"If your goods are not as you claim, I swear by Allah, I will have you whipped in this market," the sage declared coldly.

Unfazed, the trader bowed deeply and motioned him toward a worn tent. "She is my last one," the man said with exaggerated reverence. "The finest, my lord—just for you. Please, have a look."

The tasawwuf lifted the curtain and saw a girl of no more than seventeen, perhaps younger. She wore little—only a torn shirt—and her black hair, as dark as pitch, fell to her waist, partially concealing her emaciated frame. Beneath her brows burned a fiery defiance and resolve. Her hands trembled, bound to a pole by thick ropes. They had worn her wrists to raw, bloody patches.

"Why is she bound?" he asked, studying her intently.

"She has a fiery temper," the trader replied, slightly annoyed. "She attacks potential buyers, so no one wants her. I've endured enough trouble and am letting her go for almost nothing. Just looking at her hair and shape is a true source of delight! I'm sure a master like you can rein her wild nature."

The sage approached her, indifferent to the merchant's effusive praise. He wasn't interested in her physical allure but in her eyes—gateways to a soul from the distant lands of the Borysthenes. Her spirit was malleable clay, waiting to be shaped into whatever vessel he desired.

"If you discount a little for her damaged wrists, I'll take her," he said.

And so, a new concubine entered the life of the aging imam.

In the next decade, the tasawwuf could recall how he had tamed her anger and stubbornness. He had won her trust, then her devotion. He had trained her in the secret arts of the tasawwufs.

Now, the time had come to reap the rewards of his patience and effort.

Suddenly, the sage felt a presence—someone unseen was watching him, standing just behind him, uncomfortably close. The tasawwuf turned his head sharply. The open terrace, while spacious, offered no real place to hide. The only possibility lay within the chambers behind him. Could he be under surveillance? Whoever the intruder was, they would pay with their life, and Islam Giray's dogs would spend days searching for the body.

The chambers of the Khan's vizier were large and lavish. But time spent in the intriguing in the Sultan's court had honed the sage's instincts. He immediately identified several likely hiding places from which someone could spy—or strike with a blade laced with poison. One such spot was across from the terrace entrance, a small, concealed space separated by a false wall. Yesterday, it had been empty, but now...

The tasawwuf decided against exposing the hiding place himself. It was better to let the intruder reveal it. All he needed was focus.

Within moments, a figure convulsed on the cold marble floor, gasping for air. The sage recognized him instantly—Murza Davlet-Bey. This bumbling fool was about to pay for meddling in affairs beyond him. Deprived of breath by the tasawwuf's magic, the murza would soon leave this world in agony. But at the last moment, the sage reconsidered.

He knelt beside the writhing man.

"I warned you about prying into matters that do not concern you," the sage hissed. "What have you already told the Khan or the vizier, hmm?"

Davlet-Bey clutched his throat, shaking his head vehemently, unable to speak. The tasawwuf saw an opportunity—this clumsy murza could be useful after all.

"Listen carefully," the sage whispered, his voice piercing the murza's hazy consciousness. "The mace, as you know, is kept in the vizier's treasury. Bring me all the keys. If you dare deceive me again, the falcon you saw earlier will pluck out your eyes."

Chapter Eleven

Davlet-Bey did not need much time to carry out the task given by the magician. Were it anyone else, the fear of the Khan might have stopped him. But he feared the Turk more, and that fear he could not explain to himself. Likely, it was the cursed magician's spells.

The murza breathed heavily, as if trying to take in every last bit of air fate had allowed him. He kept glancing over his shoulder. The cursed Turk haunted him. He felt the Turk could read his mind and know his secrets. If caught, and publicly impaled, Davlet-Bey might have found it a liberation. His own foolishness had made him prey to a foreign will.

The stolen keys jingled treacherously with every step. The sound seemed especially loud amidst the deathly silence that filled the corridors of the vizier's mansion. Finally, as he approached the Turkish magician's quarters, now ten paces away, Davlet-Bey felt hot breath behind him. Then, a horrific stench hit him.

A sudden blow sent him sprawling to the floor. For a moment, he lay on his back like an overturned beetle, gasping for air in the darkness. Out of the shadows appeared two large, ruby-red eyes. Then, an enormous, fanged muzzle emerged, dripping foul slime onto his chest. Davlet-Bey wanted to scream, but the nightmare dissolved abruptly into the darkness. Somewhere far away, or so it seemed to him, a faint light flickered from an oil lamp near the Turk's chamber.

When Davlet-Bey finally reached the door, he noticed that the stolen keys were no longer in the shredded pocket of his tattered robe.

Yaryna had always felt safe and sheltered with her master. In the strange land where fate had cast the young maiden, that meant a great deal. Her new master was a famed warrior and a sage. He had never once made advances toward her, despite having no other women in his household. Yet one evening, the tasawwuf returned angry from the Sultan's divan and lashed out at Yaryna.

"Why does your face always look as if you're toiling away on a galley?" he barked as soon as he saw her. "Is the simple duty of washing my feet too much for you?"

Yaryna said nothing. Taking a copper basin of water, she quietly began to wash her master's feet.

"I understand well that you've lost your freedom and, perhaps, much else that once mattered to you," he continued, his tone softening. "But you are alive and healthy now, living in a land that may yet become your homeland."

Yaryna remained silent.

The sage lifted her chin gently, forcing her to look at him.

"You don't need to serve me as if you had a dagger lodged in your back," he said. "If you find your fate in my home too unbearable, you're free to leave!"

He stood and walked away, his wet, bare feet slapping against the marble floor. She simply watched him go. Maybe she really should kill him and escape? But first, she needed to win his trust.

That fateful evening, over ten years ago, Yaryna had entered the sage's room wearing only a silk robe. Since then, she'd had countless opportunities to plunge a knife into the magician's back but had never done so. Each time he embraced her, kissed her, and claimed her, she saw Ivan's face and promised herself she'd do it next time—not now.

Eventually, Ivan's gaze stopped haunting her. His eyes, his features, faded almost entirely from her memory. Then came a day when, trying to recall her loved ones, Yaryna attempted to resurrect Ivan's image but failed. That day, she wept bitterly and for a long time, begging forgiveness from both her beloved and God. Yet, when her tears dried, it seemed the restless shadows of the past receded, no longer tearing her soul apart. She was no longer Yaryna—she was Mariam.

Her silver-haired sage was always near, if not in body, then, as he claimed, in spirit. She grew accustomed to his calm, quiet voice, recounting incredible tales he swore were true.

In the foreign Tatar palace, Mariam felt uneasy. There were too many dim corners, untouched by the light of countless lamps. Even the silk sheets felt unpleasant against her skin.

Mariam sat on a low, wide divan in the room assigned to her, straining to listen. Something was about to happen. But, everything the tasawwuf had taught her over the years vanished in an instant. It was replaced by a deep, ancient fear of the inevitable.

The palace was silent. She could hear only her own breathing, which sounded loud and heavy to her.

Suddenly, in the deep silence, she heard a sound. It pricked her skin like a thousand needles and sent tremors through her body. In the adjoining room, she could hear the click of claws against stone. How had the beast gotten so close? This was the second floor; the windows were barred.

Never in her life had Mariam encountered a werewolf. What would happen if she failed to dominate its mind, as the sage had taught her? The wolf would rip her open in an instant, spilling her entrails onto the polished marble floor. She was sitting directly in its path to the coveted mace.

The heavy fabric of the door curtain stirred with a swift motion. Mariam froze, straining to see what she would face. As if in response to her desire, a set of claws slashed the curtain away, revealing the darkness beyond.

The adjoining hall was completely unlit, which was unusual. Mariam squinted, trying to discern the creature, praying the tasawwuf would arrive to protect her. At last, the beast emerged wolf with enormous fangs and glowing red eyes. It approached her slowly, barking its teeth.

She noticed the stench emanating from its maw only a little. Their eyes met.

The tasawwuf had warned her of a flood of evil energy. It would seek to overwhelm her. Instead, she felt something familiar—achingly so. It filled her soul, and she lost all control over the situation.

"Ivan, is that you?" she stammered, bewildered.

In the mental plane where they stood, the fields stretched endlessly. Scattered haystacks dotted the fields like pieces on a chessboard. Yaryna and Ivan stood side by side, gazing at each other in astonishment.

"Yaryna..." Ivan said, his voice filled with disbelief. "I thought the Poles had killed you."

"They didn't. They sold me to some pagan merchant for a pittance. Then I became the property of a Turkish magician."

"Can a person truly become someone's property, even a magician?" Ivan asked, studying her closely.

She shrugged.

"So, you're a magician yourself," she replied, turning away. "Save me, Ivan..."

He buried his face in her thick, pitch-black hair. After all these years, it still smelled of meadow herbs. Though how could there be meadows among the pagans? This thought jolted Ivan back to reality—to the awareness that all of this was but a vision.

"What are you doing here?" he asked.

"I'm here to take your power and give it to my master," she replied, her voice steady.

"Would you dare? I'm your Ivan, your love! Have you forgotten?"

"Almost..."

"That sorcerer has ensnared your soul..."

The illusion shattered. Mariam opened her eyes to see the tasawwuf standing before her. The terror that had briefly subsided surged back with a vengeance. His face, gray and corpse-like, was lit with fiery rage. In his wide palms, spheres of flame flickered, ready to unleash death. She had never seen her master like this before. He had often spoken of his magical prowess but had never shown it.

Ivan—or rather, the werewolf—was gone. He had disappeared, presumably with the mace, leaving her to face the sage alone.

"You failed me," the tasawwuf roared, his voice booming throughout the mansion. Or was it merely in her head? Paralyzed by fear, Mariam could only wait as the sage approached, bringing with him the stench of sulfur and the searing heat of hellfire.

"Mariam, why didn't you obey my command?"

She could not answer; she could barely breathe. Her lungs felt ready to turn to ash.

Then, suddenly, the infernal heat subsided. The tasawwuf returned to his human form. He knelt before her, lifting her chin with one hand. Their eyes met.

"It's not about him being your compatriot, is it?" his voice was eerily gentle. "This is the one coincidence I failed to foresee—a festering sentiment the weak call love. But I do not blame you. I'm sure your lover knows the torment I can inflict if I don't get what I want."

The sage drew a dagger, grabbing her trembling hand in his calloused grip.

"This will hurt a bit," he said, smiling darkly, "but your scream will summon your old flame. The Sultan has commanded me not to return without the mace and its power..."

Before he could drive the blade further, a low, menacing voice rang out:

"Let her go, scum!" Ivan's voice thundered. "Face a Cossack's wrath instead!"

Then Ivan appeared. His blade clashed with the magician's. A battle of steel and fire shook the Tatar palace's marble walls.

PART TWO

Petro Sobol

Chapter Twelve

The most difficult part of this trial for Petro was the rule to drink mead before his exercises. It made an already challenging task—proving himself worthy of joining the Sich brotherhood—even harder. What could be managed with focus and a clear head became almost impossible after that cursed drink. Barely able to stand, Petro would stagger up to Sirko and ask:

"Why must a future Cossack guzzle so much liquor? Isn't there another way?"

The ataman would usually remain silent for a while, puffing on his pipe and studying the young man closely.

"Perhaps you, Ataman, could put an end to this ridiculous tradition?"

"You're not to judge which customs in the Sich are foolish," Sirko would finally reply, twirling his mustache. "You'll understand why you need the mead when the time comes—if you manage to pass the trial. If not, then look for another fate."

Amid the good-natured laughter of his comrades, Petro would trudge back to his barracks to sleep.

The weeks of training on the Sich passed quickly. Petro tirelessly swung his saber, performed drills, and, even more determinedly, drank hearty mead in the evenings. Sometimes, dark visions of Rudyi's death—he should have returned long ago—flashed through his mind, but Petro tried not to dwell on them.

The other Cossacks never tired of teasing him:

"Look at young Sobol drinking like a true warrior! Maybe it'll help him pass the trial next time…"

"In drinking, perhaps? He's got a long way to go to catch up to you!"

Petro ignored the jokes. More than anything, he wanted to prove to Sirko that he was capable, so the ataman might take him on scouting raids.

Yet there was another side to his life. Late at night, when the noisy Sich finally grew quiet, Petro was left alone with his ghosts. Once he closed his eyes, his mother appeared. Her brightly colored scarf was on. She looked at him sternly, as always, when the Sich was mentioned. His father would come next, tearing off his sleeve to show his stump of an arm and asking:

"How am I supposed to hold a saber?"

In recent nights, his elder brother Stepan started appearing in his dreams. He fought fiercely against the Tatars, standing in the thick of battle alongside Rudyi and Sirko. Then he would vanish, leaving Petro standing off to the side, merely watching. When the fight ended, Petro was tasked with finding the wounded. He would always find Stepan—bloody and lying in a clearing surrounded by Tatar corpses, clutching a saber with a blade broken clean in half. Petro would try to take the weapon, but his brother refused to let go.

Petro woke up screaming and crying. Then, he wandered the narrow streets of the Sich, threading among the long barracks.

Petro had lost count of how many times he had attempted the trial. That grim morning, he decided it would be his last attempt. Wasn't it time to stop making a fool of himself in front of everyone? Even as he approached the barrel of liquor, he heard the stinging remarks of the Cossacks behind him:

"Drink up, Petro! That's all that's left from your nocturnal escapades!"

He was so furious he nearly turned around to thrash the joker. But he caught Sirko's steady gaze, as always shrouded in clouds of pipe smoke, watching him intently.

"There he is the chief mocker of gullible recruits..." Petro thought as he grabbed the barrel.

For some reason, the mead no longer affected him. Petro completed the obstacle course even faster than required. He found himself astonished—his body seemed to move on its own, as though he were merely a bystander.

Petro finished the last step. He set down the yoke with two full buckets of water. He watched as the overseers examined the sand beneath the pole he had carried.

The sand was dry. Not a single drop had spilled.

At last! Petro gave a triumphant glance at the suddenly hushed brotherhood.

"Ah, you've finally learned to control your body, as a proper Cossack should," Sirko said after the induction ceremony. He studied Petro with his usual, searching look.

"Does this mean I'll join the next battle?" Petro asked eagerly.

"You will—once you prove to me right now that you can handle a saber," the ataman replied.

"Who do I fight this time?" Petro asked, ready for another match.

He had many teachers and had already surpassed some of them. But when Sirko blindfolded himself and took up a saber, Petro felt uneasy.

He had never sparred with the ataman before. It was unlikely anyone in the Sich could rival Sirko's skill. Could this be another joke?

Petro attacked, but Sirko effortlessly deflected even the trickiest moves the young man had learned. Whatever happened, this duel didn't carry any real consequences. The worst outcome would be that

Sirko wouldn't take him on the next raid. But that couldn't go on forever.

These thoughts raced through Petro's mind as he broke out in a sweat, struggling to defend himself from Sirko's strikes. A moment later, he was on the ground, the tip of Sirko's saber pressing against his chest. The Cossack froze for a moment, then tore off his blindfold and looked closely at Petro.

"Do our enemies fight like this?" Petro asked as he got to his feet.

"Some do," Sirko answered curtly, sheathing his saber.

"Teach me to fight blindfolded," Petro said.

Sirko smiled enigmatically, picking up a metal ring and hanging it on a branch.

"Turn away, blindfold yourself, and take your saber," Sirko said. "When I give the signal, turn and thread the ring onto the tip of your blade. It will be swinging."

"How am I supposed to know where the ring is?" Petro asked, puzzled.

"You have other senses besides sight," Sirko replied. "Learn to use them."

Thus began Petro's journey toward becoming a *kharkternyk*—a path to understanding himself. The lessons absorbed him so completely that he barely noticed when Sirko and his comrades left for missions or returned. Sometimes, he didn't even know they had been gone.

One day, after several days of training beyond the rapids, Petro searched for his barracks leader, Hrudka. Everyone he asked about Hrudka's whereabouts gave him strange looks as if he were mad. Finally, he approached the scribe, a grim, gaunt old man who often grumbled about the Cossacks' antics.

"So much human strength wasted," the scribe muttered, looking up from his parchment. "You'd be better off plowing fields than swinging those swords around. You'll all die without homes, wives, or children."

Petro had never spoken to the scribe before; he respect-ted the man's education but also feared him a little.

"Sirko has dried your brains with his witchcraft," the scribe said quietly, dipping his quill into the inkwell. "Youthful hearts chase illusions, unable to grasp the wisdom of seasoned Cossacks. Hrudka died in battle with the Tatars a week ago."

Petro stared at the scribe, hoping for something more, but the man returned to his writing. Petro's fists clenched, and for a moment, he was tempted to spill ink over the scribe's bald head. Instead, he walked out silently, not even slamming the door.

It was stiflingly hot, with a storm brewing but refusing to break. Long meditation in any weather were an essential exercise for those seeking to master the art of the *kharkternyk*. Sirko often said, "It's futile to seek extraordinary power outside yourself—it must be found within."

Petro sought that power daily, but today, whether from the relentless sun or something else, he couldn't focus.

"Those who expect the world to accommodate them will always find themselves in trouble," said Sirko.

Petro hadn't even noticed the ataman approach. It rattled him, but he remained still.

"Trying to awaken a warrior's strength within while annoyed by nature is a fool's errand," Sirko continued.

"What else should I do, Uncle Sirko, when you won't let me join your raids?" Petro retorted.

"A scout who lets the heat distract him is no good," Sirko said, tying his horse to a crooked tree and sitting beside Petro.

"I knew your father and elder brother Stepan well. I couldn't keep them in this world. But with you... that's still within my power."

"A true Cossack finds his way to hell," Petro said with a grin, repeating his father's old joke.

"If you're a real Cossack, hell is guaranteed," Sirko replied, half-serious, half-jesting. "Now, take a blindfold and your saber. Let's see if you've been wasting your time."

The clash of steel echoed across the hillside as the two warriors moved with inhuman speed. Their bodies fought on the earthly plane, but their spirits battled in another realm hazy, light-filled expanse.

"At last, I can speak with you in a way no one else can hear," Sirko said.

"If we sat on the hill and whispered, no one would hear us either," Petro quipped.

Sirko's face glowed in the mist, the same light Petro saw in the spirits of his departed family during his meditations. But Sirko was alive, and this strange connection unsettled the young Cossack.

"We face an enemy who sees and hears from afar," Sirko said. "I should have known another sorcerer would pursue the mace. But the quarrels in the Sich and the Polish king clouded my mind."

"Is Rudyi dead?" Petro's heart sank, and the ethereal veil around them began to waver. He steadied himself.

"Ivan is alive, as far as I can sense. But this isn't about him," Sirko replied. "Perhaps I'll regret this in a week, but I have a mission for you."

"So, I'm ready?"

"I don't know if you're truly ready, but this task... even I can't handle it. Listen carefully!"

Chapter Thirteen

The stone walls of the Kazykermen fortress loomed high over the Borysthenes. When the sun rose in the east, the grim, gray river inlet near the docks remained cloaked in shadow, its foul-smelling waters undisturbed.

The first fortifications had cut down the surrounding trees. This left a stifling silence, broken only by the guttural cries of Tatar guards.

The stillness came to life only when a supply vessel entered the inlet. Then the fortress walls would echo with the shouts of sailors, the splash of oars, the creak of rigging, and the rumble of carts laden with provisions.

Ibrahim Pasha despised this place and considered the Sultan's command to station him in Kazykermen a sign of displeasure. The desolate location and the threat of Cossack attacks didn't bother him much. What infuriated Pasha was the necessity of dealing with the Tatars in all matters. He had hated them since childhood, when his father had served as an imperial ambassador at the Tatar Khan's court.

Ibrahim would never forget how the Khan's children would corner him in dark alleys and beat him mercilessly. This memory came unbidden as he stood before the fortress deputy commander.

The murza had an unusual appearance for a Tatar and a piercing gaze. He might have even been Turkish. Bowing respectfully, the *murza* spoke softly:

"My master sends generous blessings of Allah upon you and your descendants. He apologizes that he cannot receive such an esteemed guest in person."

"What is the reason for his absence?" Ibrahim asked, barely concealing his irritation.

"The Khan summoned him to the capital on urgent matters."

"Has the liberation of the lower Borysthenes and the Liman from the northern savages ceased to be a priority for the Khan's vassals?"

The *murza* bowed even lower, clearly adept at handling irritable guests within these walls.

Pasha studied the pristine white of the *murza*'s elaborate turban and held his tongue. He wanted to rant about the Tatar nobility's irresponsibility and incompetence. But he suspected this man might not be a Tatar. So, it tempered his anger. He almost asked where the *murza* was from and how he had ended up in this backwater, but decided it was not the time.

"I trust you understand that I didn't come here to feed the mosquitoes," Ibrahim said more calmly.

The *murza*, still bowing, gestured for his guest to enter a spacious, well-lit hall. The room was comfortable yet militarily austere.

The walls were adorned with captured weapons, and the stone floors were softened by a few luxurious Persian rugs. A meal and fine wine awaited on a table, but despite his fatigue from the journey, Ibrahim resolved not to eat until the meeting was concluded.

As he reclined on a divan, he invited the *murza* to sit as well. Deciding not to touch the wine, he asked, "Can you assure me that there are no unwelcome ears here? We will discuss matters of great importance."

"This is the safest place in the entire lower reaches," the *murza* replied.

"What is the current mood among those infidels who call themselves the Zaporozhian Army?"

"They have strength but lack the wisdom to use it," the *murza* said after a pause, watching his guest carefully. To Ibrahim, it seemed the *murza* was lost in thought even as he spoke, but oddly, he did not take offense.

"What do you mean by that?" Pasha asked.

"Since Allah removed Bohdan Khmelnytsky, local leaders dispute who should wield the hetman's mace.""

"Can our spies meet the expectations placed upon them?" Ibrahim asked skeptically. "We need someone loyal to the Porte to lead the Hetmanate. Is that clear?"

The *murza* nodded silently.

"I know there are many leaders among the Zaporozhians who are dissatisfied with the current state of affairs in the Hetmanate. Their discontent can be exploited for the benefit of the Sultan and the Porte," Pasha continued, his voice firm.

"All possible measures are being taken," the *murza* replied briefly, bowing his head again, his gaze fixed on Pasha as if waiting for something.

"About two dozen large ships are being prepared in Ochakov to sail up the Borysthenes," Ibrahim said. "They must reach here in a few weeks. Your task is to ensure their reception is impeccable—above all, secure and entirely secret. Cargo is of the utmost importance: provisions and weaponry. With these, we will crush the rebellious Zaporozhian Cossacks and place the mace in the hands of a puppet leader. Once we control his power, neither the Polish king nor the Tsar of Moscow will dare to challenge the Sultan. May Allah prolong his days."

"Would my lord be displeased if I shared my thoughts on the Sultan's plans?" the *murza* asked.

"Speak," Ibrahim said, finally relaxing enough to glance at the food on the gilded plates.

"All necessary precautions will be taken to ensure the cargo reaches its destination," the *murza* said softly. If Ibrahim had been more attentive, he might have noticed the ironic undertone. But the Pasha, inspired by the boldness of his strategy, missed it entirely.

"However, there is a problem that the planners seem to have overlooked," the *murza* continued. Ibrahim stopped chewing.

"What problem is?"

"The Liman's shallow waters make it dangerous for heavy transport and military ships. They risk running aground."

"But the loading is nearly complete," Ibrahim protested, swallowing hard as a piece of meat lodged in his throat.

"To avoid derailing the Sultan's plans, send an urgent messenger. Order the cargo transferred to smaller, flat-bottomed vessels. They are better for navigating rivers like the Borysthenes," the murza advised.

"But that would cause delays," Ibrahim objected.

"If not done, the heavy ships will become stranded in the Liman and fall prey to the Cossacks," the *murza* insisted. "You will not receive the Sultan's praise for such a failure."

The two argued in hushed tones for some time. Eventually, the *murza* slipped out of the hall and into the fortress's cold, dim corridor, vanishing in moments.

Silence flooded the space around Ibrahim Pasha. He began to feel uneasy, unaccustomed to such stillness. In his palace in Istanbul, there was always activity, even in the dead of night—footsteps, voices outside the windows, or the scurrying of rats. Here, he could hear his own breath entering and leaving his lungs, punctuated by the sharp crackle of oil lamps on the bare stone walls.

The oppressive quiet pushed him to pace the room, but the echo of his own footsteps multiplied until it became overwhelming.

It felt as though the foreign land itself sought to drive him mad, sending legions of invisible spirits to break his resolve. Could these formless foes be defeated before engaging enemies of flesh and blood? The thought gnawed at him.

Ibrahim, seeking distraction, summoned a servant. He ordered them to bring him the finest concubine in this barbaric place. To his surprise, she was far better than he had anticipated. He fell asleep only when the first rays of dawn pierced the somber walls of Kazykermen.

Upon waking, he found the woman gone but recalled their conversation vividly.

"Does my lord believe in sorcerers and evil spirits?" she had asked.

"In this wild land, you'll believe anything," Ibrahim had replied, relishing her presence.

"The *murza* sent to us by the Tatar Khan is an evil sorcerer. He summons dark spirits in his chambers and speaks with them.

Ibrahim had smiled. "How do you know this?"

"I have a keen sense for sorcerers—Allah granted me this gift. And I saw him do it once," she said.

"You spied on him?"

"It happened by chance. He had a crystal orb that glowed as he recited prayers in an unfamiliar language, like the local dialect."

"You tell an interesting tale," Ibrahim had remarked.

"I've long wondered why Allah placed me in this dreadful place. What sin have I committed? But now I understand—it was to warn you of great danger. Will my lord not show mercy and take me away from here?"

Rising, Ibrahim had scratched his bald head before donning his turban.

"Hmm... A Tatar *murza* who speaks in Sarmatian language. And I wondered why he didn't look like a Tatar. We'll have to keep an eye on him."

Chapter Fourteen

Stepan closed the heavy door behind him and, finding himself in a dark room with a lantern in hand, let out a sigh of relief. The madness he had endured was finally paying off—he had received vital information. But there was little time to act on it.

The fortress commander had likely already reached Bakhchisarai[17] and realized that the summons to the Khan's audience did not exist. His return with reinforcements was a matter of one, perhaps two days.

How resistant Pasha would be to Stepan's suggestion was uncertain. He might awaken in the middle of the night and arrest the suspicious *murza*.

Stepan needed to deliver the news about the Turkish flotilla to Sirko immediately. But sending a messenger to the Sich was out of the question. Writing it down for a carrier pigeon was too risky; the message could be intercepted. That left the most effective yet dangerous method: using magical communication with Orysya.

---

[17] The Khan's Palace or Hansaray located in the town of Bakhchysarai, Crimea. It was built in the 16th century and became home to a succession of Crimean Khans ↑

If Sirko had explained his plan to Stepan now, the latter would have called the leader mad. Every evening, as Stepan reflected on surviving another day, he replayed their conversation in his mind, wondering what had possessed him to agree.

It was winter. In the hut, an attendant tended to the stove. Stepan and Sirko sat at a table near a small window, outside of which a snowstorm raged.

"On Saint Nicholas Day in summer, the Khan's vizier will send a *murza* to Kazykermen with valuable gifts for the fortress commander—some Tatar whose name I don't recall..."

"Are the coffers of the Zaporozhian Army empty?" Stepan interrupted, tipping back his cup.

Sirko fixed his gaze on Stepan, twirling the end of his mustache around his finger.

"You make jokes now, but the fortress weighs heavy on my mind," Sirko said after a moment's silence. "The Polish Crown is also ready to help..."

"Samoylovych[18], for instance, suggests seeking aid from the Tsar of Moscow," Stepan remarked.

"What's your take on that?" Sirko asked, his scrutiny of Stepan intensified.

---

[18] Ivan Samoylovych (Ukrainian: Іван Самойлович) was the Hetman of Left-bank Ukraine from 1672 to 1687.

"You know I'm no politician," Stepan replied, "but when someone keeps saying we can't accomplish anything without the Tsar's army, it makes me sick."

"So we handle it ourselves, you think?"

"Exactly, Sirko. We can take Kazykermen, but the cost in lives will be high."

"Every giant has feet of clay," Sirko said. "We need someone on the inside."

"How many scouts have already failed to return?"

"We need more than just a scout," Sirko said impatiently. "We need a *kharakternyk*. A skilled one, with the gift of persuasion."

Stepan raised his eyes to Sirko.

"Even if..." Stepan trailed off, shaking his head. "The *murza* you mentioned will be accompanied by at least two hundred janissaries. No persuasion will work..."

Sirko finally smiled and raised his cup in triumph.

"What if we reduce your task to just three people?"

Stepan leaned forward.

"If I find anything useful, I'll rely on it through Orysya," he said quietly. "She'll pass it on to you through a messenger."

Stepan still remembered Sirko's smile under his long, smoke-stained mustache.

"I must admit," Sirko had said, "this may be the first time a woman proves useful to the Cossack cause!"

Stepan had used his powers of persuasion before, but only during interrogations of captured Ottomans. This was the first time he had to convince an enemy he was a friend. Sirko had assured him that no one in Kazykermen had seen the *murza* in person, not even the commander. But could anyone be certain in such matters?

Over a year ago, disguised as a captured Turkish nobleman, Stepan had approached the fortress gates with four janissaries. He spun a tale about a robbery along the Liman coast. Luckily, the fortress commander was simple-minded. He responded well to Stepan's influence. His favor was easily secured with a chest of Turkish treasures, which "brave warriors of Allah had saved from the barbarians." Since then, any envoy from the Khan could have exposed the ruse, but none had.

Pasha, however, was proving to be the most difficult challenge yet. From the moment Stepan laid eyes on the Turkish general, he felt the weight of danger. But alongside that danger came an unexpected boon: critical intelligence.

Stepan now had to open a magical portal to Orysya.

Orysya was a witch renowned not only in her village but far beyond. She cured grave illnesses, predicted cattle epidemics, and was said to control the weather and accelerate crop growth.

Though many secretly sought her help, no one openly queued at her tidy cottage nestled in a cherry orchard for fear of the priest's curses. Her busiest hours were always at night.

Orysya met her clients in an old, half-ruined chapel with a dark reputation. It was in a long-abandoned graveyard several miles from the village. According to local lore, a mysterious plague wiped out the village that once stood there.

Stepan had met Orysya when she was a frightened little girl, shunned by everyone. Her mother, a renowned herbalist, had kept her hidden in a forest hut until the girl escaped and fled to the village.

Starving and dressed in rags, she resembled a small demon from hell seeking a better life. No one let her in, though many secretly bought potions from her mother.

One cold autumn evening, Stepan found her crying beneath a haystack near his yard. Her wails sounded less like sobs and more like a curse upon humanity's indifference.

Out of fear more than compassion, Stepan brought her a blanket, bread, and milk. He lit a hidden fire in a nearby ravine and watched over the sleeping girl all night. Thus began their unlikely friendship.

Now, in the dim room of Kazykermen, Stepan placed the magical crystal orb on the floor and recited a prayer. A bright blue light filled the room. It transported him to the shadowy realm where he and Orysya sometimes met.

But she was not there.

On the small table where she once brewed potions lay parchment and a pen contingency plan if they couldn't meet. As Stepan scrawled his message, the hut's frail door began to rattle violently.

Something was wrong. He hurriedly inscribed his bro-ther Petro's name on the letter, ensuring no one else could decipher its meaning. He prayed Sirko would find Petro in time.

As he concealed the orb, a knock came at his chamber door. His hand went instinctively to his saber.

"Who is it?" he asked, feigning irritation.

"Ibrahim Pasha is awake and demands your presence, my lord," a soft, soothing voice replied—a concubine.

Relieved, Stepan sheathed his saber. Pasha wakes up so early after a night with such a beauty? Strange.

But when the door opened, a short, bald man with a sickly gray face and piercing eyes stood there. One hand gripped a mace; the other held the trembling concubine.

Before Stepan could react, an unseen force slammed him to the floor, paralyzing his body.

"Well, my bright falcon," the intruder said, crouching beside him, "you're exactly who I've been looking for..."

Chapter Fifteen

Petro Sobol had doubts about his understanding of Sirko's instructions. His head began to spin when the leader mentioned his older brother, Stepan. He was alive and hiding in the Tatar stronghold.

The thought that a kindred soul still existed in this world gave him wings. For three days as he traveled north, Petro couldn't stop thinking about Stepan and feeling proud.

How had he managed to outwit the infidels for so long? Now *that* was a true *kharakternyk*! In his mind's eye, Petro envisioned his brother returning to the Sich, alive and well, and the two of them fighting their enemies' side by side. These thoughts carried him to the outskirts of the village Sirko had spoken of. Now, he only needed to find the witch's house.

Imagine that—Stepan had fallen for a fortune-teller. Their father would have had a whip ready for such a revelation...

"Excuse me, good sir, could you tell me where Orysya, the healer, lives?" Petro politely asked an elderly man repairing a fence outside a large, whitewashed hut.

The old man looked up and studied Petro from beneath his thick gray brows.

"From the Sich, are you, lad?" he asked.

"Yes, sir, from the Sich," Petro replied cheerfully, dismounting and bowing as he approached.

The man stroked his long beard thoughtfully.

"My nephew left for the Sich back in Catherine's time," he said with a far-off look, "and we've heard nothing of him since..."

"I could ask about him when I return," Petro offered.

The old man brightened.

"That would be kind of you. His name is Mykhailo Hryn. If it pleases you to inquire..."

"So, about the healer?"

"She lives on that hill," the man said, pointing with a thick finger behind Petro. "But you're too late. Yanger Gudz cut her down this morning..."

"He *what*?!" Petro blurted, staring at the old man in disbelief.

"I warned him that drink would be his ruin. The lad's young..."

"That can't be true..."

"Oh, it's true, as true as God is my witness. Go see for yourself. She's lying there now, in a coffin in her house. Come back afterward; I'll fix you a good supper."

Petro was stunned. If the healer was dead, he wouldn't receive the vital information Sirko spoke of. He approached the house but hesitated to enter. In the entryway, a group of old women argued loudly about the misfortune of preparing a witch for burial.

After wandering the village aimlessly for some time, Petro returned to the old man's home. Supper was hearty, but conversation with his hosts was strained. He retired early.

Petro awoke suddenly in the middle of the night, as though someone had shoved him. The house was dark and quiet, save for the rhythmic snoring of the old man and the soft murmurs of his wife.

Petro lay back down, but sleep eluded him. He felt as though someone was standing nearby, watching. When he finally drifted off, a bloodied image of Stepan broke through his dreams.

"Did you find Orysya?!" his brother rasped.

Petro woke up drenched in sweat and bolted from the house, accidentally knocking over a water barrel in the entryway with a loud crash.

The night air was cold, but Petro sprinted toward Orysya's house, hidden in the shadows. Perhaps the healer had left some sort of message. He had to check. He forced himself not to think about the coffin the old man had mentioned.

He reached the garden. The trees swayed violently in the biting wind, shedding their leaves as though discarding a heavy burden. Twisted trunks creaked under the strain, their eerie groans resembling the eternal laments of lost souls.

Petro ducked into the small entryway. The space was cramped but warm, and it smelled of dried herbs. The heavy door to the main room creaked as it opened, revealing a soft glow of candlelight and the faint scent of incense.

The room was empty. Of course, no priest would offer prayers for a witch's soul in the dead of night.

Petro avoided looking at the coffin in the center of the room. His eyes landed instead on a large ironbound chest. It had no lock. If there had been anything of value, the old women likely took it by now. Still, he thought, who would care for scraps of parchment?

Kneeling, he opened the chest. If he were hiding documents in this house, this is where they'd be. But inside was nothing but old junk.

Suddenly, Petro felt a presence behind him, standing silently, staring. A chill raced down his spine.

Behind him stood only the coffin. His imagination conjured a vivid image of the pale which rising slowly, holding out a scroll in her stiffened fingers.

"Who better than a *kharakternyk* to outwit dark forces?" Sirko often said with an ironic smile, twirling the end of his mustache.

Would he retreat from his first battle? Turning around, Petro saw nothing unusual. Only the coffin on chairs, the pale, candlelit profile of the dead, and the faint rustling of wood beetles in the floorboards.

Petro felt a pang of disappointment. To prove himself to Sirko, he was willing to confront the dead witch. But she, it seemed, had no intention of indulging him.

Suddenly, a mournful song drifted through the garden. A girl's voice, filled with sorrow, pulled Petro toward the door.

In the darkness stood a beautiful girl in white, with a wreath on her head. She sang a haunting melody and stared unblinkingly at Petro.

Time and space faded. He saw only the girl, as if suspended in a void.

She beckoned, her hand motioning for him to follow. Then, she turned and glided away, her presence cutting through the darkness like light through fog.

Petro followed, step by step, until she vanished into thin air.

He found himself on the edge of a forest by a small pond. Yellow leaves floated gently to the water's surface, performing a final dance.

The pond began to glow, its waters bubbling. From beneath, ghostly maidens emerged, their skeletal hands tangled in weeds. They reached for him, singing the same mournful song, pulling him into the icy whirlpool...

"Enough!" a commanding female voice shattered the enchantment.

Petro screamed and scrambled out of the pond. The apparitions vanished beneath the water.

"Who are you looking for, boy?" asked an unseen presence.

"Orysa, the healer," Petro stammered, his lips trembling.

"She has gone to rest and won't return soon," the voice replied.

"But she had something to give me..." Petro managed to say.

"Who are you?"

"Petro Sobol..."

Ivan Sirko studied the young man as if seeing him for the first time. Once, that kind of attention would have been a reward, but now Petro felt like a fool.

"What happened next?" Sirko asked.

"I panicked and ran," Petro admitted. "I ended up in a graveyard, surrounded by hands reaching out of the earth. They called to me with terrifying voices..."

"You said you were in a forest?"

"When I ran, the forest disappeared, and I found myself in the cemetery..." Petro hesitated and met Sirko's gaze. "You're an experienced *kharakternyk*. Can you explain what happened in that cursed village?"

"Sounds like strong mead," Sirko said, twisting his mustache, "or maybe the herbs in the witch's house played tricks on you..."

Petro leapt from the bench, glaring at Sirko as if he were a Tatar.

"So, you think it was all...?"

"Calm yourself, boy," Sirko said with a steely tone. "Thousands of your comrades will soon march to storm KazyKermen. Polish gold and politics are involved. I must persuade Samoylovych not to beg the

Tsar for mercy. News from your brother could strengthen my case. And you tell me fairy tales."

Petro sank back, lowering his head. It was hard to argue with Sirko's words.

"I haven't touched a drop of mead," Petro muttered. "But yes, the house was filled with dried herbs... maybe I inhaled something."

The hut fell silent.

"You look terrible, boy," Sirko said at last. "Rest up. Tomorrow will be a hard day."

"I haven't slept in days," Petro replied, standing. "But last night, I finally dreamed. I saw a wide river filled with rowing ships under black sails."

"And then?" Sirko asked.

"When I flew closer to see, crows appeared out of nowhere and tore at me. Three times I woke and fell back into the same dream."

"Hmm. Your vision may hold a vital message," Sirko said after a thoughtful pause. He poured a cup of mead and handed it to Petro.

"Are you sure?" Petro asked hopefully.

"I can't be sure of anything until I see it with my own eyes," Sirko replied. "But it's worth investigating."

Chapter Sixteen

From that harrowing night when Yaryna last saw Ivan, she had been kept locked away in one of the vizier's opulent, windowless chambers. Servants with veiled faces occasionally brought her lavish meals. Heavily armed guards silently opened and closed the heavy doors. But Yaryna barely touched the food.

Once, exhausted from sleepless nights, she had allowed herself to drink. Fueled by curses against the khan, she turned the room into a wreckage of shattered treasures, awaiting death at any moment. Yet her screams, tears, and curses met only a deafening wall of indifference. Finally, she fell asleep.

When Yaryna awoke, she found three burly janissaries standing over her, their swords drawn and their eyes fixed on her. And truly, there was much to see—her frenzied state had left her fine silk garments in tatters.

She cared little for their stares. Rising to her feet, she made no effort to cover her bare chest or push the wild strands of hair from her face. The janissaries recoiled as though she were a witch who had just emerged from the depths of the northern steppe. A raw, untamed power radiated from her, a force of nature that left even seasoned warriors feeling vulnerable. They instinctively raised their blades, though she made no move to attack.

Silent, she stood there, each man convinced her piercing gaze was fixed solely on him. The chill of it reached their bones.

Now she was being led through the underground corridors, enshrouded in a luxurious Persian shawl. She had agreed to this solely for the chance to see Ivan one last time, while he still lived—while they both still lived.

He had thought the graveyard would be guarded by at least a dozen janissaries. But when Murza reached the site, there was no one.

He easily located the grave and began to dismantle it, tearing his fingers and breaking nails in the process. Moving the stones was easier than digging through the compacted clay and rubble beneath. The sharp fragments tore his hands, but he pressed on as if something in the grave was calling to him. The sea breeze carried the first hints of dawn.

Suddenly, the hardened clumps of earth shifted. From the grave's depths, a hand shot up, followed by the gray, mud-caked face of tasawwuf.

"Elixir…" the revived sorcerer croaked.

Murza had not expected to see the Turk alive, not after the dagger had pierced his back. The khan had ordered the body preserved. He would later deliver it to the Ottoman envoys. Tasawwuf had been no ordinary man. He was a trusted advisor to the sultan.

For days, tension hung over the khan's court. The murder was bound to provoke either a diplomatic scandal or war. Yet less than a week later, a secret envoy from across the Pontic Sea arrived, stating that the sultan wished to pretend tasawwuf had never existed.

The body was to be buried the following night. Keys stolen from the vizier's estate were never mentioned, and the mace was guarded by heavily armed janissaries.

It should have all ended there, like a nightmare fading with the morning. But the voice of tasawwuf echoed once more in Murza's mind, compelling him to the dungeon where the Turk's body was kept. To go there, risking accusations of treason, was madness. Yet Murza could not resist the sorcerer's overwhelming will.

For nearly a week, tasawwuf had lain in the dungeon's deepest recesses. The khan's physicians had examined the body and assured him the sorcerer was dead. The khan hesitated to desecrate the corpse, fearing the sultan might later demand proof of death.

Murza trembled as he removed the burial shroud from tasawwuf's face. The Turk's eyes stared back, alive. Murza's heart nearly stopped from terror.

"Prepare the elixir and unearth me," tasawwuf commanded weakly. "I need more time to recover. Remember the recipe..."

Even if he wished to forget, Murza knew the recipe would remain seared into his memory for the rest of his life, assuming he lived long enough to grow old.

After draining a large jug of the elixir, tasawwuf emerged from the grave. Before Murza's eyes, the Turk transformed into a massive, ravenous werewolf.

Ivan hung from the rack, naked and bloodied. At first, Yaryna did not recognize her beloved in the dim light. Then a janissary brought a torch closer to his mangled face, and she froze in shock in the middle of the torture chamber.

"Ivan?" she managed to whisper.

He did not respond. His body hung limp from rusty chains, as though life had already left him. Tears streamed down Yaryna's face. Had she endured ten years of slavery only to find her beloved destroyed in a pagan dungeon? Should she have driven the Turkish blade into her own heart when she had the chance?

She took a step forward, sank to her knees before Ivan, and began to weep.

A tall shadow appeared behind her.

"Turkish sorcerers are astonishingly ignorant of the ways of ordinary people," came a rasping voice, its mocking tone a fresh wound. "They wandered deserts for years, seeking power in human nature. They return, arrogant and powerless against a simple woman's feelings.""

Yaryna froze. Hatred burned away her tears.

"And I marvel," she said, her voice trembling with fury, "that anyone thinks they can break a Cossack with mere torture."

"Clearly, you've spent too long in the comforts of the sultan's palace and seen too few dungeons," the shadow replied smoothly. "Otherwise, you wouldn't be so naive."

"You've already tortured my beloved to death. What more could you possibly want?"

"Your Cossack is alive," the shadow retorted, and Yaryna whirled around to face Ivan. "He can endure much before his soul departs. But you are correct: without you, his suffering is meaningless. No matter how much pain he endures, he cannot give me what I desire."

"What do you want?"

"The same thing your dead master sought. Take his power and give it to me. I'll spare both your lives."

"Life will mean nothing if you wield the mace's power..."

"But are you prepared to watch him suffer endlessly?"

Silence fell. The shadow loomed behind her, its gaze heavy and suffocating. Could she lunge at this phantom, sink her nails into its throat before the guards struck her down? She would end it all—but only for herself. What would become of Ivan?

"I agree," she whispered.

The shadow solidified into the figure of the Tatar khan. He seized Yaryna by the shoulders, spun her to face him, and brought his face close to hers.

"I knew you wouldn't resist," he said coldly. "But if you try to deceive me, I will make you both watch each other suffer for days."

A guard appeared, his torchlight revealing a face pale with fear.

"Did you bring the mace?" the khan demanded.

"The mace is gone, my lord," the guard stammered, nearly prostrate on the cold stone floor.

"What do you mean, gone?" The khan's fury erupted as he grabbed the janissary by the collar. "Who took it?"

"No one knows, my lord. The locks are intact..."

"Execute everyone guarding the treasury!"

"Yes, my lord, but..."

"What?!"

"My men dared to check the Turkish sorcerer's grave..."

"And?"

"It was unearthed. Empty."

Even in the dim torture chamber, the khan's face betrayed a flicker of confusion, quickly masked by rage.

"What nonsense is this? Who would steal that charlatan's corpse? Even if someone did, they couldn't have gone far..."

Suddenly, a shadow flitted silently to the corner of the room.

Gripping an axe, Yaryna lunged at Islam Giray, her hair wild and her eyes blazing with fury. She looked like a ghostly revenant.

The janissary reacted swiftly—her frail body crumpled under his crooked blade. The heavy axe clattered to the stone floor, dark blood pooling around her lifeless form.

Even in death, her wide smile remained. Ivan Redhead stirred, his shattered eyelids lifting to fix on Yaryna's frozen smile. A guttural moan, almost a roar, tore from his chest.

The khan glanced indifferently at Yaryna's corpse before turning his attention to the reviving Cossack. He snatched the torch and addressed the janissary.

"If you don't find the mace by week's end, I'll have you impaled like the pagan dog you are," he snarled, then left.

Yaryna saw a clear sky, its expanse framed by the gnarled branches of an old willow. She and Ivan had often watched sunsets here, near her modest hut by the forest. Those were happy days when they breathed life deeply and dreamed without care.

Ivan's voice echoed in her mind:

"As soon as Ostap the miller finishes his new mill, I'll start work right away. Then neither my father nor my mother can object to our wedding…"

"And what sort of life will that be, Ivan," she had teased, "when your parents glare at me like wolves?"

He would block the sky with his frame, gaze into her eyes, and say earnestly:

"We'll find a way, Yaryna. My father promised us a plot by the pond. I'll build us a white, cozy house, and you can decorate it however you like."

"When will that be…" she would reply, her youthful smile full of hope.

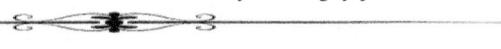

They would sit in silence until the sun sank. Then, they would reluctantly part, still holding hands, until her mother called her home.

Now, the forest hummed softly in the twilight, each tree like an old friend. Ivan's uneven breath filled her senses, both comforting and unsettling. His presence was as real as the janissary's blade in her chest and the blood soaking the grass beneath her feet.

Chapter Seventeen

Ivan Samoylovych sat at the table in the ataman's kurin[19], his head bowed over a goblet. Though he seemed drunk on mead, the hetman was sober. His attendant had filled the cup, but it remained untouched. Inside him a storm raged no drink, however strong, could quench.

The door creaked open almost inaudibly. From the cold darkness outside, the figure of Sirko appeared. He hesitated for only a moment, but Samoylovych noticed.

"Come in, I don't bite," the hetman said, lifting his head.

The ataman stepped inside and shut the door firmly. The kurin was unheated, cold, and damp.

Samoylovych rose, poured a second goblet, and offered it to his guest.

"I know you'd prefer to act without my help. But, the council of elders still holds some sway here on the Sich, doesn't it?""

---

[19] Kurin (Ukrainian: курінь) is a type of housing, sometimes temporary, which can vary in size and purpose: from a small tent made of leaves, to a large wooden house for permanent occupation.

Sirko downed the strong drink in one gulp, a faint smile curling under his smoky mustache.

"No one on the Sich questions your authority as hetman..."

"And yet, today's council decided that you, Sirko, as ataman, will lead this siege of Kazykermen," Samoylovych replied, barely restraining himself. "What is that, if not defiance of the council's decisions?"

Sirko sat on the bench and twisted his mustache around his middle finger.

"They would have chosen the Samoylovych who fought the Muscovites and drove them from our lands," Sirko said. "But Samoylovych who stands before them today proposed uniting with Moscow to defeat the Turks.""

The hetman leapt at his feet, lunging toward Sirko as if to strangle him.

"What goes through your mind when you plan the siege of Kazykermen?" he demanded in a hoarse voice, staring the ataman down. "I'll tell you what I see: a mountain of your comrades' corpses! It's you who'll bury them, you who'll look into the eyes of the maimed. Is that what you want?"

Sirko frowned and lowered his head.

"I know what you're getting at," he said, "but when I see moscovites[20] garrisons in Kyiv and Poltava, do you know what comes to

---

[20] Same as "russian"

mind? Not the ruins of our women's homes where Muscovite soldiers were billeted and fed. Not the confused faces of farmers whose hard-earned bread was stolen to feed the Tsar's insatiable army. I see you—dead—on the gallows. That is the fate awaiting anyone foolish enough to trust the Muscovites!"

Samoylovych recoiled as if he had truly seen himself with a noose around his neck. He sank back into his seat.

"Spare me the fairy tales, Ivan," he muttered. "Tell me instead how you plan to repay the Polish king for his gold."

"The fortress isn't ready for an assault yet..."

"And neither are we," the hetman grumbled.

"My scouts report that a Turkish flotilla will soon sail from Ochakiv to the fortress. It is loaded with provisions, weapons, and reinforcements," Sirko said, as if speaking to himself. "I'm considering intercepting them in the estuary. After that, Kazykermen may fall into our hands without a fight..."

A loud knock interrupted him. Before either man could respond, the door burst open, letting in a blast of autumn air. A disheveled Cossack staggered inside, his coat torn, his trousers caked with mud. While the attendant hastily stoked the fire, the unexpected visitor sat silently on the bench, removed his boots, and hung his soaked coat near the stove.

Samoylovych watched the scene in astonishment before speaking.

"Look at how lax your discipline has become," he said.

"What do you mean, Ivan?" Sirko asked, puzzled.

"Is it common practice for anyone to barge into the ataman's kurin and dry their boots?"

Sirko's expression hardened. His brows knitted, and he shot a sharp glance at the hetman.

"First, not anyone—a Cossack of the Zaporizhian Host. "My comrade," he said with conviction. "Second, this is Mykola, a scout from the far southern outpost. If he's here, he has something to report."

"Let's hope his news is worth drying boots by the ataman's fire," Samoylovych replied with a sneer.

Sirko said nothing, though his clenched jaw betrayed his irritation.

The scout, meanwhile, acted as if no one else were present. After draining a goblet of mead, he stared into the fire for a moment before quietly speaking.

"Four Bashi-Bazouk cavalry detachments are advancing quickly in this direction. Infantry and artillery wagons follow close behind."

"What devilry is this?" Samoylovych muttered, but the others ignored him.

"The khan marches on the Sich to distract us from Kazykermen," Sirko said calmly, twisting his mustache. Deep lines furrowed his brow.

"We must meet the khan's forces head-on," the hetman said, his gaze narrowing. "And we must do it far from this place."

"And we can't let the Turkish flotilla reach the fortress," Sirko murmured thoughtfully. "But there aren't enough men for both tasks."

"Perhaps I lack the finesse to earn the trust of your esteemed Sich council," Samoylovych said with biting irony. "But even you must admit the necessity of involving Muscovite troops in this matter."

Sirko acted as if he hadn't heard and turned to his attendant.

"I asked you days ago to find young Sobol. Why hasn't he reported to me?"

"He hasn't been seen on the Sich for nearly a week," the attendant replied without looking up from his task. "They say he went off searching for a fortune-teller…"

Sirko clutched his head.

"What the devil is going on here?" he muttered in despair. Without another word, he grabbed his saber and stormed out into the cold autumn night.

Heavy pounding echoed at the door, accompanied by muffled shouts. A crowd had gathered outside, sensing that something strange was afoot.

Tasawwuf felt the power he had drawn from the Cossack scout coursing through him, healing his dagger wound and filling his veins with fire. Gripping the mace, it seemed as though molten energy had replaced his blood. He wrapped the mace in his cloak and glanced at the scout's lifeless body, its eyes burned black.

The Turk's gray, contorted face bore a rictus of agony. Blood pooled beneath him, mingling with that of the slain servant girl. Doing such a ritual with an ordinary woman was a risky gamble. It was especially so given the scout's growing potential as a sorcerer. But there had been no other choice.

Freed from his grave on the city's outskirts, tasawwuf had transformed into a wolf to steal the mace from the treasury. Exhausted, he had hidden in nearby caves. Consuming human flesh had sustained him for a time, but traveling to Istanbul in his weakened state remained impossible.

He had turned to his master's secret art, sending his consciousness into a great raven. The bird soared northward, searching for the distinctive power of a sorcerer. The raven circled safely above the Dnipro estuary, wary of venturing too close to the Sich.

Finally, the bird detected a potent source of energy emanating from within Kazykermen. Whether it was a captive or not hardly mattered. Gathering his remaining strength, tasawwuf prepared for the journey.

At midnight, atop a wind-swept crag, a massive wolf appeared. Throwing back its head, it howled long and loud, filling the night with an eerie, chilling cry.

Chapter Eighteen

The fire had nearly burned out, and most of the men had returned to their quarters. A few remained, their legs too unsteady from drink to carry them anywhere. Only one figure sat by the embers, feeding them kindly, and he seemed sober. It was Petro Sobol. Ever since his return from his last mission, he'd barely slept, fearing the return of a dream he dreaded seeing again. Not the one about the ships, which he had shared with Sirko, but another dream he didn't even want to remember. Yet, he sometimes wished ears were willing to listen.

In the dream, Petro ran through a dense forest that seemed to claw at him, trying to ensnare and topple him. He fell, rose, and ran again. The forest gave way to an ancient graveyard, its tombs unmarked by crosses. Hands of the dead clawed out of the ground, trying to drag him under. Each step grew heavier until the earth seemed ready to swallow him whole. In his final moments of struggle, when his strength was nearly gone, a strong hand grabbed him and pulled him onto the grass with one swift motion.

He found himself in an open field. Nearby sat his brother, Stepan, his head resting on his knees. He was motionless, his clothes soaked with sweat and blood as if he had come from a fierce battle.

Petro rejoiced to see him alive. He called out, but Stepan didn't respond. Petro touched his brother's shoulder with hesitation, only to find it hard as stone. Suddenly, Stepan raised his head. The face that looked back was twisted with pain; his eyes replaced by dark, empty hollows. Petro screamed and awoke in terror.

"Help me..." Stepan's voice echoed in his head throughout the day, filling him with pain and dread. What could he do? How could he help? If Stepan was still alive in the fortress, the dream meant one thing: his brother was in grave danger. Someone had discovered him and was torturing him. The siege preparations were underway. But, who could guarantee reinforcements would arrive in time? For Petro, Stepan had already died once. Could he let it happen again without speaking to him about their father, their mother, their village?

"Why aren't you sleeping?" a voice interrupted his thoughts.

Petro looked up to see old Myshko standing in front of him. Myshko was known as a man of immense strength, one who could, according to rumor, catch bullets with his teeth.

"Uncle Myshko," Petro began hesitantly, "I've heard you have some kind of miraculous potion that heals even the gravest wounds."

"Yes," Myshko replied, stroking his beard, "but it's been gone for nearly a week. I gave the last of it to someone and haven't had time to gather more."

"I heard that potion is made by a sorceress who lives nearby," Petro continued. "I could fetch some if you tell me where to find her. We'll need it for the coming battle. What do you think?"

Myshko shrugged. "Why not? I'll tell you where she lives—it's an important task. But be sure to return by tomorrow evening."

"Of course, Uncle Myshko," Petro said, already moving to saddle his horse.

Nearly every village in the Hetmanate had its healer. Usually, she was an old woman with a face like a wrinkled apple, piercing, faded eyes, and disheveled gray hair. No one could say how long she had lived there or who her parents were. Everyone simply assumed she had always been there. These women gathered medicinal herbs and roots. They dried them on their rooftops under the scorching July sun. Then, they brewed potions using secret recipes. These recipes were never written down. They existed only in memory, destined to fade into the same infinity that claimed their lives.

The sorceress of this village, nestled on the northern borders of the Great Steppe, was no exception. Locals simply called her "the hag," for no one knew her name, and she never mentioned it. Her modest, whitewashed cottage stood in the village's heart. A dozen similar homes surrounded it near the church, along with an orchard of gnarled apple trees.

People visited her not only for healing potions but also for fortune-telling or to seek charms for love or protection. Occasionally, they begged her to halt the sudden deaths of livestock. She was even summoned as a midwife, though the local priest disapproved.

When Petro dismounted at the gate of her yard, no one paid him much attention. Cossacks were a common sight in these parts. He entered through the open gate and surveyed the scene. Plump chickens pecked for grain in the yard. A goat grazed on the last tufts of yellowed grass by a doghouse. The tip of a shaggy tail protruded from the doghouse. The dog didn't stir at the stranger's approach.

For a moment, Petro doubted he had come to the right place. But when the mistress of the house emerged onto the porch, his doubts vanished. Thick, not-quite-gray hair hid most of her face. Only her piercing eyes were visible. They could belong only to a true sorceress.

Petro greeted her with a polite bow. The old woman hobbled closer, leaning on a cane.

"I've lived long enough," she said, not greeting him. "I've noticed something peculiar about human nature: the living is overly concerned with the dead." Many would be shocked to know how little the dead care about the affairs of the living. When your journey ends, you're weary and all you want is rest. Let me assure you, young man, it's unpleasant when someone you've left behind—someone dear—holds you back between worlds, trapped by their passions."

"My brother needs help," Petro said quietly. "He calls me every night, but I don't know how to reach him. Please, help me!"

The old woman softened slightly. "As I see it, your brother didn't accomplish something he considered important in life. His soul now wanders, seeking release from the burden it created for itself."

"Then how can I help him?" Petro pleaded.

"I'm too old to guide you there myself," the sorceress replied, lowering her gaze. "But you, as I've noticed, have the skills of a sorcerer. I'll show you the way…"

Petro followed the sorceress's instructions. The ritual she described sounded like a drunken Cossack's campfire tale. He buried bones beneath a withered tree by a pond and recited an incantation. When he finished, nothing happened. Frustrated, he gathered wood, lit a fire, and cooked a rabbit he'd caught during his search for the tree. The meat was tender and flavorful.

Sated, he built a small shelter against the autumn winds and fell asleep, regretting he hadn't brought a flask of mead.

He awoke to the sensation of someone's presence. Something soft tickled his forehead. Opening his eyes, he saw long, luxurious hair. Startled, he sat up to find a girl in a white blouse sitting beside him. Her dreamy face basked in the warm rays of morning sunlight that had found its way into the hollow.

Petro felt the chill of the night in his bones but remained still, afraid to scare her away.

"This summer was warm and long," the girl said, her voice filled with melancholy. "Just like that year…"

"Are you lost? Cold?" Petro asked, draping his coat over her shoulders. "I can take you home."

She finally turned to him with a bewitching smile.

"If I could leave, I wouldn't need your help to find my way."

Though her voice was soft, it sent a shiver down his spine. Petro studied her closely but saw nothing unusual except the deep sadness in her gray eyes.

"What holds you here?" he asked after a pause.

She pointed to the withered tree. "That rope... but perhaps not only that."

"How could it possibly hold you?" Petro asked skeptically.

"My mother called me Kalyna. I don't remember my father," she began, her sorrowful gaze fixed on the dead tree. "As I grew up, I became the village's greatest beauty. Almost every lad circled me at gatherings, which, I suppose, meant I had to do without friends," she added with a wry smile. "But it was Taras, the son of the wealthy Chumachenkos, who captured my heart. A handsome, dark-haired boy, even younger than me. Unlike the others, he never flirted or even greeted me, he didn't dare. But I could feel his lingering gaze. I would smile at him, though he wouldn't respond. He just kept looking. That cursed gaze—it burrowed into my soul."

Her voice softened as she continued. "We grew closer at the winter evening gatherings. He was shy and quiet, which made him seem dull to most. But I enjoyed spending long winter evenings with him. Mostly, we sat in silence, and he just stared at me. It seemed like he wanted to say something but never did. In spring, his parents forbade me to go near him, claiming I was corrupting their son and distracting him from his duties. In truth, they had found him a bride from a wealthy family. Before Ivan Kupala Night had passed, the matchmakers were already knocking at her door."

Kalyna's voice faltered as she stared at the ripples in the pond, created by the rain beginning to fall from the gray void overhead. "Through it all, Taras and I met here in secret, watching the sky reflected in the water. It's just like the sky above is colorful and bright. Walking into the water feels like stepping into the heavens."

She paused, letting the raindrops fall unbidden from the sky, blending with her story's growing melancholy. Petro, unaware of the cold wind biting at him, leaned forward, impatient for her to continue. "What happened next?" he asked, spellbound by her voice and temporarily forgetting why he had come.

Kalyna looked at him as though seeing him for the first time. "What happened? My Taras promised one night he'd leave everything behind, and we'd run away together. One warm July evening, he did what he'd wanted from the start," she said. Petro noticed her cheeks were wet, whether from tears or the rain, he couldn't tell. "I didn't resist because I wanted to give myself to him completely. The next evening, it happened again, and the next, and the next—an entire week. The village must have been abuzz with gossip about us, but I didn't care. Nothing mattered to me."

Her tone darkened. "Through it all, my mother never said a word. When I snuck home late at night, she was always awake, waiting in the corner by the icons. Then it ended. One night, I came to meet him, but he didn't show him. The next day, as I worked in the yard, children pelted me with rotten apples, screaming 'whore!' before running away. After Taras's wedding, life became hell. We locked ourselves in the house, too afraid to step outside."

Kalyna's voice grew quieter, tinged with regret and sorrow. "My mother never scolded me, but I saw her health deteriorate rapidly. Within a month, she was bedridden. I handled the chores alone, though I don't know where I found the strength. I learned to ignore the neighbors' scorn and the children's cruelty. Then, one night, she passed away in her sleep. I discovered her lifeless body the next morning. It was then I realized I was pregnant. I can't recall much of what I did after that. I remember only despair and rage. I blamed myself for her death. I begged for her forgiveness through tears, and then, consumed by fury, I destroyed everything in the house, screaming until my voice broke. Those who saw me then—wild-eyed, disheveled, in a dirty shirt—thought I had lost my mind. And they said so to my face, with no pity, only satisfaction: 'Serves you right.'"

She straightened her posture, her voice filled with bitterness. "The morning after her funeral, I took a rope and came here. Back then, this tree was alive. But after it absorbed all my grief, it withered."

Kalyna turned her tear-filled eyes toward Petro, her expression burning with hatred. "Everyone who watched my burial believed I deserved it," she said, her voice now hoarse. "Tell me, young man, would it be so unjust if the Turks or the Poles came to this village and razed it to the ground?"

Petro remained silent. Fear gripped him, not just of this girl, but of her despair and fury. In that moment, his only wish was to vanish, to escape her presence. Yet could he truly leave without seeing his brother?

Kalyna fell silent, as though she had read the young Cossack's thoughts.

"You'll get what you came for," she finally said. "But for that, I demand payment."

Stepan appeared just as Petro had last seen him, preparing to leave with their father for the Sich. He wore a white, embroidered shirt their mother had sewn, bright crimson trousers, and new boots bought on a family trip to Poltava, thirty versts[21] away.

"Why are you just standing there, little brother?" Stepan's voice broke the stillness. "Aren't you going to come over and embrace me?"

Petro was so startled that, at first, he couldn't speak. His heart ached to run to his brother, to throw his arms around him, but Stepan stood in the middle of the lake, on the water itself.

"There's an abyss between the worlds of living and the dead," Kalyna had warned. "Those who dare to build bridges over it are destined for ruin. The dead call out not to destroy the living, but because their souls are restless, seeking refuge in the grief of those left behind."

"You called for me, Stepan," Petro finally found the courage to respond. "And here I am, before you."

---

[21] A verst equal to 1.0668 kilometres (3,500 feet).

"Did you receive the message I sent through Orysia?" his brother asked.

"I did," Petro replied, "but not through her. She was already dead."

Stepan lowered his head, as if crushed by an unbearable weight of sorrow. He sank down onto the water's surface, and ripples spread out from where he sat, forming a foamy chain that lapped at Petro's feet.

"Don't despair, Stepan," Petro said, trying to console him. "You'll see her again. Father and Mother are waiting for you, too."

"I know, Petro, I know," his brother answered, his voice heavy with resignation. "I long for that reunion, but before I go, I must tell you something."

"I'm listening," Petro said.

"My life was taken by a powerful sorcerer wielding a magical mace—the very one Sirko has been seeking for so long. I wasn't ready for that fight and allowed this great power to fall into the hands of an enemy. That sorcerer now travels along the left bank of the Borysthenes toward Ochakiv[22]. If Sirko acts quickly, he can reclaim the mace. He's the only one who can. But if he fails, the Sich and all the Hetmanate will fall beneath the sabers of the Tatars or even the Ottoman Sultan. Neither the Polish King nor the Russian Tsar will save us then."

---

[22] Ochakiv located in place, where the Dnipro River meets the Bug River. The Ochakiv fortress would be a long-contested place due to its strategic location.

In the Chumachenkos' yard, musicians had been playing since morning. Their daughter was marrying some Moscovits she had met while studying in Kyiv.

The Chumachenkos were the wealthiest family in the village, and everyone sought to stay in their good graces. Nearly two years had passed since their son Taras ruined the life of a poor girl, and no one spoke of it anymore. Many owed the Chumachenkos money and feared having such a powerful family as enemies. Rumors swirled that they were close to the regiment's scribe himself.

As for their daughter, she had been the subject of endless gossip. Every eligible young man in the area had pursued her at some point, but her prospects were few. Raised in finery brought from Kyiv and Krakow, she had standards far beyond what most could meet.

The village which had been invited to the wedding. The bride's mother had come personally the day before, bringing gifts and pleading for her presence, fearful of any ill omens on such a day. After all, when the scandal with her son Taras had erupted, she had done everything in her power to ensure no lasting harm came to him. Now, for the first time in years, the old witch was attending a wedding—not as a guest, but as a silent observer.

As the bridal party returned from the church that afternoon, the witch sat quietly at the table in the expansive courtyard. Around her, guests feasted and celebrated, but she neither ate nor drank, merely watched, sensing something was about to happen.

When a young Cossack entered the yard, the witch recognized him immediately. It was the same lad who had visited her the previous day. She had a sinking feeling that her actions had unleashed something she could no longer control.

The Cossack moved through the crowd, speaking quietly with the guests, who pointed him toward the manor. A short while later, Taras appeared on the high porch. The Cossack rose from his seat and walked toward him with deliberate slowness. The witch could only watch, helpless, as the events she had set in motion unfolded.

Taras knelt in the middle of the street; his face was bloodied. Crimson streaks ran from his nose, dripping onto his trembling chin.

"Tell me how you ruined Kalyna," Petro demanded. The words felt foreign, as though they were spoken by someone else.

"I... I loved her... my mother, she... I didn't mean for it to happen..." Taras stammered through tears.

"Don't believe him, Petro!" Kalyna's voice echoed in his mind, sharp and relentless. "He only wanted to use my body. He never cared for my soul. Punish him for what he did!"

A wave of hatred consumed Petro. It was more intense than anything he had felt before, even when the Tatars slaughtered his father. He drew his saber.

"Don't you have anything to say for yourself, anything besides lies?" he growled.

"I... I'm sorry it happened that way," Taras sobbed. "Please, don't kill me. I have a wife... a child... please, spare me!"

"What are you waiting for, Petro?" Kalyna's voice sliced through him like a blade. "Didn't you promise to do whatever it took to see your brother? Now is the time to pay your debt!"

Petro's arm raised the saber above his head.

"You'll never understand what Kalyna felt as she walked to that lake to leave this world," Petro said softly. "Let your parents and your wife feel that pain when they receive your head as a gift."

A gunshot rang out. Pain shot through Petro's arm, and the saber clattered to the ground. Before he could react, a rider appeared and struck him with the hilt of a pistol, knocking him to the ground.

Petro and Sirko sat on the familiar hill where Petro had trained to become a skilled sorcerer. Since Sirko had dragged him from that cursed village, neither had spoken a word. The ritual to free Petro from the dark power had left the young Cossack drained.

"Do you know why there are so few sorcerers left, and why soon there will be none at all?" Sirko finally broke the silence.

Petro shook his head.

"Every day, lads like you come to me, asking to learn the craft," Sirko said with a faint smile. "Most don't make it far and remain ordinary Cossacks. Some, like you, find themselves on the brink of an abyss they don't understand. And rarely, very rarely, do I manage to pull them back."

"I'm deeply grateful, Uncle Sirko..." Petro began, but Sirko raised a hand to silence him.

"I tell you this not to earn your gratitude. Teaching you is its own reward—I made a promise to Ivan to be a father to you. So, I beg you, in honor of your father's memory and of Rudyi, one of my finest warriors, strive to be the last sorcerer for as long as you can."

Petro rose and bowed deeply. "I will honor your guidance, Uncle Sirko. I have no one left but you. But Stepan left me an urgent message."

Sirko's gaze sharpened.

"He was killed by a Turkish sorcerer wielding the magical mace. My brother said only you can defeat him. But I don't know how you'll find him..."

Sirko leapt to his feet as if stung. "Why didn't you speak sooner, fool? The mace isn't a needle in a haystack. Wolves know wolves from afar."

With that, the ataman mounted his horse and galloped away. Petro sat back down, ignoring the cold wind and approaching rain. A faint smile crossed his lips.

"Well, Uncle Sirko," he murmured, "we've saddled the devil this time."

Chapter Nineteen

Ivan could hardly distinguish the pounding of the drum from the beating of his own heart. The Cossack moved in a fog of weariness, performing the required motions almost instinctively. Only the overseer's shrill whistle occasionally pulled him back to reality. With it came pain. Everything hurt—from the torture he had endured to the grueling weeks of labor on the galley. But most unbearable was the agony in his injured leg, chained and weighed down by a heavy shackle that followed him like a serpent after its prey.

The air on the rowers' deck reeked of sweat and the rot of mangled bodies. This galley was a purgatory for slaves and captured Cossacks nearing the end of their days. Next to Ivan sat a gaunt man with a broken nose and a missing eye. He talked endlessly about the Wild Steppe, where he claimed to have been born. Neither Ivan nor the other rower beside him paid any attention. Each man was locked in his own shell, conserving the last drops of life within his battered frame.

Every Cossack knew how to row, having sailed many times in their small, nimble chaikas[23]. This made captured Cossacks highly valued as galley slaves. After some rudimentary training, they were sent to man the war galleys. Rumors circulated that a fleet carrying provisions and weaponry was headed toward a fortress on the banks of the Borysthenes. Ivan's current galley was one of several escorting supply ships bound for Kazykermen. He had pieced together this information from snippets of conversation among the janissaries. They often visited the rowers' deck, their weapons clinking as they lashed the exposed backs of the Cossacks with whips. Ivan had already received several such lashes before the galley had even left the port of Ochakiv, though he barely felt the pain. He mechanically followed the rhythm of the drum, gripping the oar with relentless determination.

Through it all, Ivan's mind fixated on a single image: Yaryna's pale, lifeless face staring at him with empty eyes. He still wanted to believe it was only a fevered nightmare. Occasionally, the vision of a dignified Tatar in ornate robes would intrude, standing before him and declaring:

"Your power has abandoned you. The Turkish sorcerer destroyed it. Now your place is here, in the galley. Let us see what you can do without your devilish tricks."

A signal to cease rowing broke Ivan's dark thoughts. Finally, a much-needed break. The rowers straightened their stiff backs and

---

[23] Chaika (чайка). Type of boat, used by the Zaporozhian Cossacks.

wrapped bloody, blistered palms with filthy rags. Someone behind Ivan muttered a hopeful prayer for a drink of water. It was promised back in Ochakiv, yet no one had tasted a single drop since departure.

Half an hour passed. The galley remained stationary, but no water came. Instead, a group of janissaries descended onto the rowers' deck. A tense silence fell—would the whips fly again? Many backs had already turned into bloody, festering wounds that attracted swarms of flies.

One of the Turks strode among the rows, scrutinizing the gaunt faces. Fearing he was searching for a new victim, the men lowered their heads, avoiding eye contact. Yet the Turk forced each man to meet his gaze, lifting their chins with the butt of his whip and asking the same question:

"Are you from the Sich?"

The rowers shook their heads. They knew the janissaries hated Cossacks. Torture awaited anyone who admitted their origins.

Ivan observed all this through his one good eye as he bandaged his shackled leg. Most of the men on the galley were, in fact, from the Sich. Yet, broken in spirit, they denied the title they once wore with pride. They clung to a faint hope that their brothers might pay their ransom. If the infidels didn't know who was who, why volunteer the truth?

Who could blame these poor souls? Perhaps only those who had endured the agony of the stake in a public square, dying horrific deaths before hundreds of enemies. But they were gone now, their voices silenced. Yet someday, one of them might return from the other world to remind the living of their duty to the dead. Perhaps this would happen to one of these rowers—if he survived. He might sit on his porch years later, pipe in hand, reminiscing about his free Cossack days, when a voice would whisper in his heart:

"Brother, did you avenge me? Did you make the infidels pay for my suffering?"

But not everyone is destined to hear that voice.

"I am a Cossack of the Zaporozhian Host. So what?" Ivan suddenly declared, his voice firm as he rose to his feet, despite the low ceiling forcing him to stoop.

The janissary approached, tilting his head to look Ivan in the eye.

"A year ago, your comrades killed my brother," the Turk said coldly. "Since then, I swore to Allah that I would destroy three hundred Cossacks to avenge him. I've already killed over two hundred, and they all begged for a quick death while licking my boots."

"Your brother likely died in battle," Ivan replied evenly, "and you seek vengeance through torture? Is that worthy of a true warrior?"

"Few deserve an honorable fight," the janissary retorted, tucking his whip into his wide leather belt. "I know most of these rowers are from the Sich, but only you have admitted it. Perhaps I will give you the chance to die like a real warrior. Remove his chains!"

When Ivan was led to the upper deck, he saw the Dnipro estuary stretching before him. The fresh air and open space made his head spin. How long had he spent in Tatar dungeons? Beyond the crowd of golden-leafed trees, the red-yellow sun timidly peeked out, as if embarrassed to witness the execution of one of the last sorcerers, purely for the horde's amusement.

The janissaries resting on the aft deck noticed Ivan and began shouting, pointing fingers at him. They resembled cats discovering a larder full of provisions. The janissary who had brought Ivan barked a harsh command, and within moments, everyone on the deck gathered in a circle. Someone threw a saber at Ivan's feet real Cossack saber, likely taken from the dead or surrendered. Ivan hoped it was the former, though war rarely allowed such idealistic fantasies. War was no stage for heroics; it was a one-man show starring death. Death, a masterful actor, always left an impression: excruciating pain, severed limbs, mangled bodies, shattered heads with lifeless eyes, captivity, humiliation, and torture. And blood, endless blood.

The saber's hilt was damaged, making it slippery in Ivan's wet hand. At first, the janissary attacked slowly, savoring the moment under the jeering laughter of the onlookers. He assumed the captive was too weak to pose a threat. Ivan also held back, studying his opponent's weaknesses, knowing he had only one chance to strike—his strength wouldn't last beyond that.

Just as Ivan prepared for a final desperate lunge, he froze. Behind the janissary, in the midst of the sweaty, stinking crowd, he saw her—Yaryna. She stood there like a pearl in the mud, her dark eyes piercing his soul. "Come on, Ivan," her gaze seemed to say. "Avenge me. What are you waiting for?"

Her face was as pale as moonlight, glowing eerily. She parted her lips, and a thin, dark-red trickle of blood ran down her chin. Ivan tried to focus on the fight, but he couldn't tear his eyes away from the vision. The longer he stared into her not-quite-living, not-quite-dead eyes, the more a storm raged within him. Hatred pooled from the darkest corners of his mind, merging into a powerful black tide that swept everything away, leaving his soul in ruins.

With a cry of anguish, Ivan charged at his opponent, but his saber slipped from his hand. A crushing blow sent him sprawling onto the deck.

"Wait for me, my love," he whispered through bloodied lips. "I'll be quick..."

A cannon shot echoed in the distance, followed by another. Ivan felt the deck shudder—perhaps a cannonball had struck the hull. The janissaries scattered, shouting orders. Only Ivan's foe remained standing over him.

"Pick up your oar or die," the janissary roared, his voice barely audibles over the chaos. "I've never given a Cossack prisoner such a choice!"

Ivan smiled faintly. "Then don't wait," he replied. His entire world at that moment was the slender figure of Yaryna, standing on the deck.

The janissary snorted in contempt and raised his saber high. "Die like a dog!"

But Yaryna vanished. Gunfire roared, the sound of dozens of feet stomping echoed across the deck, and a cacophony of guttural voices filled the cool night air. Foreign words flitted about like startled sparrows, chaotic and sharp. Shouts rang out—orders to prepare for a defense against the Cossack chaikas. Nearby, someone screamed for faster cannon loading. Everything was happening, except for Yaryna. Ivan had almost forgotten that he was a man marked for death.

Suddenly, something heavy fell directly onto him. It was a janissary whose head had been torn off by a cannonball. For a moment, Ivan lay motionless beneath the convulsing body, drenched in the torrents of enemy blood. Then, clarity struck like lightning. His thoughts rallied, driving away the tempest of emotions. Somewhere near the stern was the gunpowder magazine. Back in Ochakiv, Ivan had seen barrels and cannonballs being hauled there. The intensity of the artillery fire from the eastern shore of the Liman had waned slightly. His comrades were likely preparing to board the supply ships. If this galley exploded, it might give them an edge.

Shoving the corpse off, Ivan rose unsteadily to his feet, grabbed a saber, and ran toward the stern, careful to avoid the Turks' notice. His body, soaked in blood, made it easy for him to feign death if necessary. But such subterfuge wasn't needed. Amid the chaos of battle, no one paid him any attention. As Ivan approached the magazine, he saw it teeming with janissaries. They were busy hauling cannonballs and filling powder pouches, all the while chattering.

Suddenly, a nearby explosion scattered heavy cannonballs in all directions. Panic erupted. The janissaries rushed below deck, shouting and scrambling. From the sounds of water sloshing below, it seemed a breach had opened in the hull. Only two guards remained at the magazine. There was no time to think—he had to act or retreat. Emerging from the shadows, Ivan moved like a wrath, silently approaching one of the guards and slitting his throat in a single precise motion. As the man collapsed with a gurgle into a pool of his own blood, the other, who had been fumbling near a powder barrel, drew a pistol and fired. The small room quickly filled with acrid smoke.

By some miracle, the pistol's spark didn't ignite the gunpowder. Clutching his wounded shoulder, Ivan crouched by the fallen guard, rifling through his clothing. As always, the needed item was in the most accessible spot. The powder haze stung his eyes, but it provided cover, allowing him to remain unseen for a little while longer. He needed to locate a cannonball with a fuse before reinforcements arrived.

Fighting the urge to cough, Ivan lit a long fuse attached to a cannonball and stashed it among the crates...

Chapter Twenty

The breath of the Borysthenes was felt by anyone traveling to these lands in late autumn. The sharp autumn wind carried damp and cold air from the river, piercing to the bone and generously pelting travelers with dead leaves. Ancient trees groaned in lament for what might be their last summer. Young, flexible saplings sang cheerfully with the mischievous wind.

As the sun attempted to hide behind the half-bare trunks, two figures emerged on a small clearing. They moved cautiously, creeping forward. They scrutinized every bush, searching for a missing companion.

The man leading finally halted and turned to his companion. "Gryts, why are you so sure we'll catch it?"

"That beast tore apart my godfather's goat," Gryts replied. "We can't let it go unanswered. Tomorrow, Myshko, it'll come to your yard."

"We saw a wolf carcass on the way," Myshko countered. "And we've wandered too far already. Let's stay here for the night, and return at dawn," he added in a tone that brooked no argument. "Maybe it wasn't a wolf but the neighbor's dog that killed the goat. Or perhaps your godfather slaughtered it himself and forgot. The man is in his eighties, after all."

"You think it's funny, don't you?" Gryts said, though he didn't argue further.

"No, Gryts, it's not funny. It's freezing," Myshko retorted. "Let's get a fire going quickly. We've got that fox you shot earlier to feast on."

As the expertly skinned carcass sizzled under the licking flames, Myshko picked up Gryts's weapon and examined it closely.

"Hm... this is a genuine French arquebus with a wheel-lock mechanism," he concluded, casting a jealous glance at his companion. "Your uncle probably bought it off a wealthy Pole; Tatars don't have anything like this."

"You know everything, don't you?" Gryts muttered, his gaze fixed stubbornly on the surrounding darkness.

"Of course, I do—more than you, that's certain," Myshko retorted.

"You'll ruin this treasure soon enough. Sell it to me while you still can. My old musket, inherited from my grandfather, is on its last legs..."

"Here we go again," Gryts grumbled. "Why don't you think of a way for us to hunt that damned wolf faster!"

With a sigh, Myshko laid the arquebus down on his coat and picked up a knife. After cutting off a juicy piece of meat and tasting it, he grunted in satisfaction. He then pulled out a small flask in a wicker case and two cups. "If my uncle had lived on the Sich..." Myshko began dreamily, feeling the warmth of the strong drink burning its way down his throat.

"You don't have an uncle," Gryts interrupted, pouring the next cup.

"If I did, I'd understand weapons better than you."

"Did you hear that?" Gryts suddenly choked on a piece of meat.

"Hear what?"

Both hunters immediately sensed another presence.

"Something's moving—and it's getting closer," Gryts said, grabbing his arquebus. Myshko followed suit, lighting the slow match on his musket with a flint.

A massive, fanged muzzle emerged from the shadows into the flickering firelight.

"Holy Mother of God..." Myshko breathed, pulling the trigger. Two shots rang out simultaneously. For a few moments, the air was filled with the haze of gunpowder smoke.

"Did you hit it?" Myshko asked, fumbling with his powder flask. "I aimed right at its jaws. Why aren't you answering?"

Turning his head, Myshko found not Gryts, but the same monstrous maw. Its bloodied fangs glinted like forged steel. The wolf advanced on him; its red eyes gleaming as it examined its next victim. Gryts lay nearby in a pool of blood, his throat torn open.

Throwing down his unloaded musket, Myshko stumbled back, unable to tear his gaze from the beast. But it relentlessly crept closer.

Pressing his back against a tree trunk, Myshko's trembling fingers searched the leaf-covered ground for any stick or weapon, to no avail. He screamed, but the sound was drowned by the stench emanating from the predator's jaws.

A shadow flitted behind the poised attacker. In the next instant, something dark and heavy knocked the wolf off its feet. Myshko could only see the light of the fire in the clearing. The air around him filled with deafening growls, snapping branches, and the crunch of teeth. Leaves, grass, and chunks of earth flew into the air like shrapnel. Then, silence fell. Even the wind stilled, joining the petrified man in awaiting whatever horror might come next.

A bright moon crept cautiously into the black sky, casting a pale-yellow glow on the clearing. Into the center of this glow stepped a massive shaggy beast, its eyes blazing with blue fire. It stood on its hind legs, raised its head to the moon, and let out a long, haunting howl. Then, before Myshko's astonished gaze, the creature began to shrink. Within moments, it transformed into a man clad in Cossack attire. Then, just as suddenly, it vanished.

An hour passed before Myshko dared to rise and approach the site of the transformation. Other than Gryts's bloodied corpse, there was nothing to be found. Picking up his musket, he was about to flee toward the village when something unusual caught his attention.

Under the canopy of a sprawling beech tree, where the pale moonlight didn't reach, lay a massive, dark form. Perhaps it was the beast the shapeshifter had slain. Curiosity took hold of Myshko. Reloading his weapon, he imagined dragging the carcass to the village and recounting his heroic battle alongside Gryts.

His legs carried him toward the dark shape under the thick trunk. Stepping closer, Myshko recoiled at the sight of bloodied fangs in the creature's maw. To his horror, he thought he saw faint wisps of steam rising between its teeth, as if the soul of the beast were leaving its mutilated body in search of a new host.

At that moment, Myshko felt someone's presence. The sparse hair on his balding head stood on end as he turned to see a gaunt man in tattered clothes standing nearby.

"Do you have any water or bread for a weary traveler?" the stranger asked, his piercing gaze fixed on Myshko.

"What the devil brought you here…" Myshko muttered, eyeing the stranger warily. Finding nothing unusual about him, he exhaled in relief. "Did you see that? It killed my friend, but I gave that monster a thrashing…"

The stranger smiled strangely in response.

"If you go hunting, be prepared to face a devil," he said.

"A devil?" Myshko asked, confused.

"Such a beast as that," the stranger clarified. "So, how about some water?"

"I've got no water," Myshko replied, casting a suspicious glance at the man. "I've nothing for you."

"That's where you're wrong," the stranger said. Before Myshko could react, the man pressed a finger to his forehead. A blinding flash of light erupted in Myshko's vision...

Chapter Twenty-One

He had lived far longer than any sage at the Sultan's Divan might dare. At times, when Tasawwuf could not sleep, faces and events from the past floated before his eyes. Countless faces and innumerable events—both good and ill. Yet as the years wore on, he could no longer discern which outweighed the other. What once seemed catastrophic now seemed a blessing in disguise. But things that once brought joy now felt like dead leaves, crushed beneath his new body's feet.

Still, some memories remained unchanged. The sorcerer recalled, in detail, a gloomy day. His mother had brought him, a six-year-old boy, to a reclusive Sufi who lived deep in the mountains.

They had secretly sold their mule for a pittance to avoid their creditors. So, the journey took three unbearable days on foot. His father had recently died, leaving behind not an inheritance but a mountain of debt. Threatened with slavery, the boy's mother had to act. She gathered what little she could and set out at midnight with a drowsy Muhammad in tow. She ignored his questions and tears, gripping his small hand tightly as she pressed onward through the darkness.

At sunrise, they would hide in caves, as they had no money for lodging. For three days and nights, his mother did not utter a word. When Muhammad spoke to her, she would only offer a weary smile and stroke his head. It brought no comfort. The boy believed his mother had gone mad and that they were doomed to perish in the foothills—of hunger, thirst, or at the claws of wild beasts.

The final night was the hardest. They ascended steadily, battling the biting wind that tore at their resolve. When the sun finally rose over a neighboring peak, an elderly man with a piercing gaze appeared before them. His shaved head was wrapped in a turban, and his gaunt frame was draped in a rough tunic of burlap.

Muhammad's mother bowed deeply to the stranger, kissed her son on the forehead, and turned to leave. He tried to follow her, crying out, pleading, but strong hands held him back. All that remained with him from that moment were the damp traces of his mother's tears on his brow. Even now, Tasawwuf could sometimes feel that moisture on his skin.

The Sufi was an extraordinarily ancient man. For the first few months, he forced Muhammad to fetch water from the spring, clean the cave, and prepare gruel from roots. The boy rose early each morning and was only allowed to rest after the sun sank behind the peaks.

Two or three times, Muhammad attempted to escape, wandering the mountains until hunger and thirst left him unconscious. Each time, the Sufi found him and carried him back to the cave.

Years of training washed away in the tides of passing decades. Yet, the Sufi's lessons on existence, life, and death remained in his memory. They were for his future Ottoman sorcerer.

Shortly before his death, the Sufi shared one of his most closely guarded secrets. Tasawwuf still remembered the old man's frail, rasping voice:

"I have taught you all I know, but I withheld one thing for this moment. "Not because you were unready. But I had to confess my wrongdoing and seek your forgiveness for my selfish intentions.""

"What could my master possibly have done wrong?" Muhammad asked.

"When your mother brought you here, I decided at once that your young and vibrant body would be my next refuge."

"What do you mean?" Muhammad did not understand.

"Once, I too was a helpless child sent to study under a Sufi master. He taught me a lot, but some things I discovered on my own. For instance, how to transfer my soul into another body."

"How is that possible?" Muhammad asked, skeptical.

"I stumbled upon a hidden cave my master had concealed for years. It was filled with scrolls. Bit by bit, I found ways to extend my life indefinitely."

"Then why haven't you used this knowledge?"

"Life in this world is wearying to the soul," the Sufi replied. "I am ready for rest. But for you, the ability to transfer your soul to another body may one day be useful. Listen carefully…"

Much water has passed under the bridge since then. By the time he became a secret adviser at the Sultan's Divan, Tasawwuf had refreshed his memory of the soul-transfer ritual. It was common knowledge that the closer one got to the Divan, the closer death crept. While he had no immediate need to use the knowledge, the sorcerer always kept the spell in mind, unsure if it would still work after centuries of disuse.

His encounter with the Cossack shapeshifter had been a complete surprise. The character was unlike the weak, unlearned fools he had dealt with before. Yet his defeat lay elsewhere. When Tasawwuf attempted to use the magic of the mace against his enemy, it inexplicably slipped away, like sand through his fingers. Feeling his life force drain, he discarded the mace, but it refused to leave him, siphoning his energy to the last drop.

Summoning an immense effort of will, he created the illusion of his own death to buy time to transfer his soul into another body—one that had been cowering in the bushes, paralyzed with fear. What followed was surprisingly simple. Tasawwuf easily overcame the feeble resistance of his new host and quickly absorbed its memories to assimilate into its life.

As he paced the dark forest, his thoughts solidified into a plan to claim the magic of the mace for himself...

Chapter Twenty-Two

Petro was one of the first to spot the Tatars: their round faces, narrow eyes beneath peculiar, pointed hats. They were short. So, on horseback, they looked like stout young lads, barely squeezed into their chainmail. This was the enemy vanguard. They were not expected to be near the Zaporizhian Host's borders. There was no time to hide—battle was inevitable. Petro cursed under his breath.

"What's the matter, Sobol? Saw a busurman[24] and soiled yourself?" came the voice of a wiry, sinewy Cossack who approached on a spirited mare. He wore only bright crimson trousers cinched with a wide belt holding a pistol, his hand resting on a saber. The seasoned warrior smirked at Petro as though the enemy wasn't even there.

"You'd better think about the beating we'll get from Sirko when he finds out we let the enemy spot us," Petro retorted, checking the locks on his pistols.

"No point thinking about it," the Cossack replied. "Let's focus on staying alive first."

---

[24] Busurmans were Muslim invaders, originally the Ottoman invaders, at least in the region near and around Ukraine

"True enough," Petro agreed. There were fewer than twenty in their reconnaissance unit, while the Tatar vanguard had nearly twice as many. Facing those odds, the wrath of their ataman no longer seemed so terrifying. The messenger was already on his way, and a warm reception awaited those red-faced invaders.

Was Petro afraid? Likely, yes. As a boy, when he had asked his father about war, his father had said, "Fear is a strength that helps you win. The key is to master it, not be its slave." Back then, young Sobol didn't understand those words; how could one control fear? What exactly was he afraid of? Pain, capture, torture, death? Sirko had often taught him how to avoid capture. But death? For a fleeting moment, Petro saw Kalyna's face. He could almost feel her breath again, the scent of her body, like oak branches and spring blossoms…

When the horde drew near, their ululating cries filling the air, Petro drew his pistol and took aim at the closest rider. His hand barely trembled.

They sat by the pond where they had first met, savoring the cheerful chirping of birds in the crown of an ancient oak.

"Strange," Kalyna finally broke the silence. "I thought that tree was dead. Do you remember, Petro? It didn't have a single leaf back then—just a rope with a noose."

Petro shrugged off his coat and draped it over Kalyna's slender shoulders. A storm was blowing, and a cold wind stirred over the water.

"Forget about that dead tree, Kalyna," Petro said gently, brushing a dark lock from her delicate face. "It's gone now. I planted this oak in its place so we could sit together and watch the birds fly in from the south, building nests high in its branches, raising their youth. Have you seen how funny they are, opening their little beaks wide, waiting for their parents to feed them?

Kalyna remained silent, forcing a faint smile, but tears streamed down her cheeks. They fell to the ground in large drops, transforming into blood. Finally, she investigated Petro's eyes and asked, "But what about the rope? What did you do with the rope?"

"Why worry about the rope?" Petro tried to comfort her, but he could see the despair clouding her gaze.

"That rope still holds me, Petro!" she cried. "It holds me tight, and I can't break free from its noose. Save me, Petro! Save me!"

Petro woke abruptly as someone shook him by the shoulders. But it wasn't Kalyna—it was a young page.

"Petro, wake up," the boy said urgently. "Ataman Sirko wants to see you."

Sobol stood up, but pain made him cry out. His torso was tightly bandaged, and a bloodied shirt lay nearby.

Wordlessly, the page handed Petro a large cup of mead. As he drained it, the memories of what had happened returned.

He had managed to take down two Tatar riders with his pistols. Then, drawing his saber, he blocked an enemy blade. Someone had struck the enemy's horse, and the dying beast collapsed with its rider, nearly crushing Petro. He leapt aside just in time and found himself face-to-face with an older Tatar, who charged at him, mouth agape and scimitar swinging.

But Sirko's training had not been in vain. To Petro, the opponent seemed to move sluggishly, as if stuck in tar. A single thrust, and the Tatar fell dead.

To an observer, had there been one amid the chaos of battle, it might have seemed that Sobol moved so swiftly that it was impossible to follow him. Enemy riders were thrown from their saddles as if by some unseen force.

Petro himself felt only an icy chill in his body, as though the January frost had descended upon him. He might have had the strength to annihilate the entire Tatar unit single-handedly, but then he saw Kalyna and froze, as if turned to stone.

She stood in the midst of the battle wearing only a simple shirt. The hot breath of death swirled around her, tangling her disheveled hair, trying to draw the black despair from her. Kalyna reached out to Petro with both hands, whispering something with her blue lips.

The vision lasted only a moment, but it was enough. A Tatar bullet struck his shoulder, and an enemy blade slashed his right side. Everything disappeared—the battle, the Tatars, the dust, the faces of his comrades. Petro found himself by the pond, beside Kalyna...

Sirko lay pale as death, wrapped in a warm blanket. At first, Sobol thought he was already gone. The senior Cossacks stood around him, shifting awkwardly. They were in the presence of hetman

Samoylovych and two Moscow officials at a table, who murmured to each other. When Petro entered the ataman's tent, the distinguished guests did not even glance his way. But Sirko immediately beckoned him closer.

"You see them?" Sirko whispered. "Already plotting who will take my place over the Sich."

"They're wasting their breath," Petro replied. "You have many years left to live, Ataman. To lead us into battle."

"Kind words, my friend, but misplaced. My final battle with the Ottoman sorcerer has drained me."

"Surely you claimed the mace, Ataman?"

The senior Cossacks hushed Petro, shuffling their feet and coughing loudly.

"God forbid they learn of the mace's power," Sirko murmured. "Without its magic, the Sich and Hetmanate will shed more blood from this alliance with the Moscow Tsar than from Turks and Poles combined."

"I don't understand, Uncle Sirko…"

"Listen carefully," the ataman said, gripping Petro's shoulder as he sat up. "I claimed the mace but destroyed it to keep it from falling into enemy hands."

Sirko glanced toward Samoylovych and his companions.

"Then Uncle Rudyi died in vain," Petro muttered, disheartened.

"Nothing is ever in vain," Sirko replied. "When I pass, do as I say, and the Cossacks will overcome any foe."

"What must I do?" Petro asked eagerly.

"Cut off my right hand and carry it with you into battle."

"Uncle Ivan, are you in your right mind?"

"Do as I command, boy," Sirko said firmly. "Before I destroyed the mace, I took a portion of its ancient power and concentrated it in my right hand. That power will kill me. But what is my life compared to the survival of an entire people?"

The dead tree stood motionless above the pond, a stark contrast to the teeming life around it. Petro approached the massive trunk and swung his axe. A dull thud—a faint tremor. Another blow. Then another. The sharp blade bit persistently into the petrified flesh, scattering splinters around. At last, unable to withstand the onslaught, the tree groaned like a weary man and toppled onto the tall, yellowed grass. But Petro didn't stop, continuing to hack the corpse into logs.

Sobol worked so fervently with the axe that he didn't notice a man descending into the ravine. The stranger stood silently, watching Petro for a long time. Finally, the young Cossack tossed the axe aside and sat down to rest. Feeling eyes upon him, he turned and leapt to his feet as if startled by an anthill. Before him stood Ivan Rudyi.

"Uncle Rudyi, is it you or your ghost?" Sobol asked, eyeing the man warily.

Rudyi smiled beneath his graying mustache.

"When you let go of the dead, the living will return to you."

PART THREE

The Witch's Path

Chapter Twenty-Three

The wound caused intense pain, and Petro felt so weak that he struggled to hold his saber. What worried the younger Sobol even more was how his comrades would react to yet another injury. Despite his youth, he had spent almost a year on the Sich as a skilled kharakternyk. An unholy force seemed to protect him from death. But now, it seemed that protection had failed. Could it be that Sirko's hand had lost its power?

When Petro shared his doubts with the old scribe, he trusted the man more than anyone else. The scribe gave him a long look, as if staring at a madman. Then he said, "Ah, Sirko has stuffed your head full of nonsense, lad." Only the Blessed Virgin, our protector, can save you from a bullet—and even she doesn't always succeed."

"What should I do, Uncle?" Petro pressed, rubbing his wound. "How can I explain this to the brotherhood so that they'll still follow me into battle as eagerly as they did under ataman Sirko?"

"Why are you asking me?" the scribe snapped. "I'm no *kharakternyk*, just a scribe."

"Who else should I ask but you? Rudyi has gone off to join the registry."

The scribe gave Petro a hard, thoughtful look.

"Don't carry a grudge against Rudyi, lad. Life is rarely as simple as it seems. Sometimes you must make hard and unpleasant choices. It's better to negotiate with the Poles now than fight them, for the strength of the Zaporizhian Host isn't what it was in my day."

"How can it be otherwise when the regimental officers in the Hetmanate either grovel to the Poles or wait for handouts from the Muscovite Tsar?" Petro exclaimed in frustration, slamming his empty cup on the table.

The scribe sighed and shook his head wearily.

"Let me tell you this, and you can decide whether to listen to an old cripple or not. The brotherhood follows you against the enemy not because they're inspired by a dead hand but because they respect you and believe in your skill. Return Sirko's hand to Sirko."

Lately, such conversations have become frequent. But they brought Petro no peace. He couldn't confess a deeper truth to the scribe. Kalyna still came to him, draining his strength and agility in the heat of battle and robbing him of peace in the dead of night. Sometimes she appeared alone; other times, she came with Stepan. Both spoke to him, even shouted, but he couldn't hear them no matter how hard he tried.

The old, rotting tree by the pond had been cut down and burned, its ashes scattered over the Dnipro. Prayers had been recited in church. Services were ordered from the priest. Several witches were paid for their help. Yet, peace continued to elude Petro's soul. He had resolved to visit the witch who advised him to deal with Kalyna. But, something always got in the way.

Petro's grim thoughts were interrupted by the fresh spring air that suddenly blew into the hut through the open door—a page had come in to tidy up. "There's a matter at hand," the young man said hesitantly. "A man has come, asking to join the Sich."

"So?" Petro asked, annoyed.

"He brought the skin of some strange beast. Says he killed a werewolf on his own."

"Anyone can boast nonsense," Petro replied. "Let him walk the plank with buckets, and the brotherhood will decide whether he's worthy of joining the Sich or just spinning tales in a tavern over a drink."

"Maybe so," the page agreed. "But many think you should take a look at the beast. It's said to be unlike anything ever seen along the Dnieper."

In the center of the square stood the punishment post, where offenders against the laws of the Sich were sometimes tied. Those who passed by were required to strike the offender's back with a whip at least once, so the square was usually deserted during such times. But today, the punishment post was empty, and near it stood a stout man surrounded by a crowd. Hands on his hips, he wore a new shirt, wide crimson trousers tucked into polished boots, shiny, given the dust hanging thick in the air.

It seemed that everyone on the Sich considered it their duty to elbow their way to the front to glimpse the enormous, fanged maw of the mysterious beast. Meanwhile, the man who owned the trophy scrutinized each onlooker intently.

The square buzzed with noise as Cossacks pointed at the stranger and his trophy, joked, and debated how the creature had been killed.

Finally, one of the elders raised his hand, and silence quickly fell. Turning to the stranger, the elder asked,

"Honored guest! The Sich brotherhood wishes to know how you managed to hunt such a fearsome beast."

The man studied the elder's face for a long time, as if searching for something, before finally replying,

"Look at it yourself and tell me—could an ordinary man track and kill such a monster? I shot it by chance, protected by the Blessed Virgin."

At these words, the crowd murmured approvingly, until someone shouted, "Maybe you crushed it with your belly instead of shooting it, eh?"

The Cossacks burst into hearty laughter.

"Show your face, jokester, so I know who I'm talking to," the hunter replied calmly.

Petro stepped forward, ignoring the man as he examined the trophy. "What weapon killed it?" he asked. "To pierce such skin from a hundred paces, you'd need a musket..."

"Or point-blank with an Austrian rifle," the stranger added.

Petro looked up and scrutinized the man from head to toe. The crowd fell silent, sensing an intense exchange.

"A good hunt is no reason to join the Zaporizhian Host without trials," the elder finally broke the tension. "If the guest is ready to prove his skill to the brotherhood, we invite him to return in a week, for now the Sich faces a *Black Council*[25] to address urgent matters."

As the Cossacks dispersed, Petro heard the stranger speak. "You must be Sobol, whose unit has been terrorizing the Tatar outposts in the Wild Steppe lately."

"Every Cossack here has enough skill for that," Petro replied without turning. He wanted nothing more than to be alone again, to dull the pain of his wound with a drink.

"In my village, they call me Myshko," the stout man said, dragging the trophy behind him. "I've heard much about Cossack valor and seen it with my own eyes many times. But rumors are spreading in the

---

[25] Black Council (Ukrainian: Чорна рада) wasa council (rada) of Ukrainian Cossacks in which participated a large number of ordinary Cossacks, as well as local commoners

Hetmanate that some Orthodox fighters rely on unholy forces to win their battles."

"The world is full of rumors. Only idlers and fools listen to them."

"Well said, lad. May the Blessed Virgin grant me another meeting with you. Farewell!"

Petro stopped and watched Myshko walk away. The lifeless eyes of the mysterious creature stared at him.

Chapter Twenty-Four

He burst out of the hut as though it were on fire, grabbing a barrel of water and tipping it over himself in one swift motion. The icy water clamped down on his head, momentarily stealing his breath, but the relief was immediate.

Petro had dreamt that he was once again in the house of the slain witch, rummaging through a large chest. Among the clutter, his eyes fell upon a golden cross on a blood-stained cord. He recognized it instantly—it was Stepan's pendant, one he had never parted with. The tarnished metal glimmered ominously in the flickering candlelight. How had it ended up in the witch's chest? Had the witch stolen it from Stepan, along with his soul?

A chill swept through Petro's body as he felt a presence nearby. He wanted to turn and look but found his neck stiff, as if it turned to stone. Clutching his brother's cross tightly, he pressed his dry lips together. Summoning every ounce of his will, he turned around.

The witch, her disheveled gray hair cascading over her shoulders, sat in a coffin, staring at him. But her gaze seemed to pierce through him, searching for something in the eternal darkness outside the window.

"Where is Stepan, your brother?" the pale lips of the dead woman moved so slowly that each word felt like an eternity. Petro fought to resist her demonic charms.

"That's exactly what I wanted to ask you," he said, gripping Stepan's cross so hard that its edges cut into his palm. The pain helped him keep his wits. "You bewitched his soul, dragged it to hell with your sorcery, didn't you?"

"We parted ways in the shadowy thickets of the afterlife," the witch replied. Her voice echoed eerily in the empty, incense-scented room. It filled the air with sorrow that made it hard for Petro to breathe. "Now we wander in search of each other, and we will find no peace until we're reunited. Our souls are bound together."

"What do you want from me? Petro asked.

A scroll appeared in the witch's skeletal hand as if from nowhere. She extended it toward him.

"This is a message from me to Stepan. When you see him—give it to him."

"You think, you devil's shadow, that I'll play messenger for you?" Petro spat through gritted teeth.

"Do it!" she thundered. Her face was suddenly inches from his own, and Petro felt himself falling into the black void of her eyes. He awoke with a start, leaping out of bed.

It was hard to say what had frightened him more—the dead witch or the abyss into which he had fallen.

The indifferent night gazed down at the Sich with the cold, eternal eye of a full moon. A light breeze carried the moist freshness of the Dnipro, yet Petro felt as though he were suffocating. He tried to draw a deep breath, but it seemed that only dust filled his lungs. The dry weather of the past week had left everything coated in a fine layer of grime. Dust was everywhere. It coated boots, horse hooves, and sweaty skin. It ground between teeth and settled in the huts like a gray shroud.

Petro glanced around. His horse stood tethered to a post, lazily chewing young spring grass alongside the others. The dark huts huddled together. Their chimneys sent smoke skyward like cats flicking their tails. The straight streets between the buildings now felt oppressively narrow to Petro.

Darkness lurked in the heart of those crossroads and squares, waiting for him to sleep again. It would creep into his unguarded mind, dragging his Orthodox soul back into the abyss.

Perhaps he shouldn't have walked the path of a *kharakternyk*. Perhaps then, he would sleep more soundly. A year had passed since he met Rudyi, yet it felt as though an entire lifetime had swept past his eyes. If only someone—Uncle Ivan, Sirko—had hinted at the darkness that would take root in his soul.

Petro suddenly realized that the Sich had become too small for him. This patch of land, now a fortress, felt like a cage. Insidious, unseen enemies constantly schemed within it. Petro longed for open spaces. He wanted to see the Milky Way in the unlit night sky. He wanted to feel the wind in his ears, hear his horse's breath, and sense the comforting weight of a saber at his side.

If Sirko hadn't been killed by the mace, if Ivan Rudyi hadn't been trapped in a web of Hetmanate diplomacy, and if one of them had been with Petro that night, they might have told him something. The darkness he faced within himself was an inseparable part of his soul from birth. There was no escape from it. If someone had told him that, perhaps Petro would have stayed by the fire, drunk a cup—or three—and gone to sleep. But he was alone. Even the old scribe slept, unable to offer him wise counsel.

As night melted away, like butter in a hot pan, and the stars receded into the morning twilight, a lone rider left through the northern gate. The Sich watched him go with the indifferent gaze of its watchfires.

Chapter Twenty-Five

The witch stood on the porch in only a shirt. She nervously thrust a candle on Petro's face. She meant to either frighten him or get a better look at him.

"I've been waiting to pull some sense into your empty head," she finally said.

"Really, Granny, something came over me at that wedding," Petro replied in a conciliatory tone. "But Kalyna still haunts me. Help me again, there's no living with that cursed specter."

"And your witchery tricks didn't work, eh?" the old woman sneered. She lowered the candle but still didn't invite the Cossack into her house.

"That Kalyna of yours sure is persistent..."

"Kalyna has nothing to do with this," the witch sighed. "You've gotten yourself tangled in something bad, lad, and now you're dragging me into it too."

"What are you talking about?" Petro asked, confused.

"Exactly what I said. Ever since that wedding, the whole village has been snarling at me because someone saw you come to me beforehand. They threatened to burn my house down. Look what's left of my barn," the old woman said, pointing her extinguished candle stub at the charred remains. "I might've ended up begging in the streets this year if not for a gentleman from the neighboring village. He promised to rebuild the barn if I helped him with you."

Petro stepped back in surprise.

"So, it was you, old hag, sending me those nightmares to drag me here on my knees?"

"God forbids!" the witch exclaimed, terrified. "I only told him about you..."

Petro's hand flew to the hilt of his saber.

"Cool your temper, Cossack," came a familiar, sly voice from the darkness behind the witch. "It's unseemly for a Sich warrior to raise his blade against a frail woman."

The old woman shrank back, clearly more afraid of the voice than of Petro's saber. Clutching the candle to her chest, she disappeared inside. Taking her place was the stout figure of Myshko.

"What do you want?" Petro asked.

"Come inside. Don't turn down what little hospitality I have—taste some of my fine vodka. Then we'll talk about business."

Petro cautiously sat on a bench near the table under the icons. The dim candlelight reminded him of his nightmares. Before him stood a brimming glass, but he didn't touch it. Myshko drained him in one gulp.

"Start by telling me who you are and what you want," Petro said. "Then we'll get to the vodka."

Myshko sat across from him and poured himself another. The small, shabby hut reeked of dried herbs, and the silence was nearly suffocating. From behind the curtain near the hearth came a faint murmur—the witch was muttering a prayer, though whether to God or the devil, Petro couldn't tell.

"There's not much to tell," Myshko began. "You saw the beast I brought to the Sich?"

"I did."

"When we found it, my godfather was killed right before my eyes. By some miracle, I managed to shoot it."

"And?"

"Since then, my godfather hasn't left me," Myshko continued, downing another shot. "Not just in my dreams—I see his bloodied, pain-twisted face everywhere: while hunting, tending to my land, even when I'm with my wife..."

"Why did you come to the Sich?"

"When I realized I was losing my mind, I decided to visit the witch. She told me there's only one way to rid myself of the specter— a journey along the Witch's Path. But the journey is perilous for an ordinary man. The old woman says no one has ever returned from it. To survive, you need to fight the unclean forces with their own power.

After Sirko's death, only you among the Sich Cossacks possess such power."

"What are you talking about?"

"Don't play dumb, lad," Myshko said. "I'm talking about the ataman's legacy. The witch told me you're plagued by the same curse as I am. Let's go together."

Petro forced down his vodka shot.

"If what you say is true," he said, "I'll go with you. But Sirko's legacy has already returned to him."

"But..."

"What kind of *kharakternyk* am I if I can't defeat a cursed ghost without the ataman's right hand?!"

Petro slammed his fist on the table with such force that the nearly empty bottle fell and shattered on the floor. The sharp shards skittered into the dark corners of the cramped room like frightened rats.

Tasawwuf gazed at the Cossack through Myshko's weary eyes but said nothing.

Chapter Twenty-Six

Stepan Sobol sat atop a tall tower, staring at the bloodstains on his shirt. His eyes welled up, yet instead of tears, blood streamed down his face. He could not remember how he got there or what had happened before. The only memory lingering in his mind was Orysia's cramped hut with its cold earthen floor. In his ears echoed rhythmic thumps, either from the feeble door, his weary heart, or perhaps distant drums beneath shaggy clouds.

What came next? His memory failed him, but Stepan knew something terrible and unexpected had occurred. Suddenly, by his foot, he noticed a large rat with wet fur and a long, hairless tail. Standing on its hind legs, the creature trembled—perhaps from cold—and studied him with tiny, blinking black eyes. Stepan was desperately hungry, yet the very thought of catching and eating the rat filled him with revulsion. Sensing danger, the rat vanished between the cold stone slabs, but Stepan's hunger remained, gnawing at him. Fighting weakness, he stood.

All around stretched a grayish, milky haze. Through a gap in the mist, the Wild Steppe stared back with an eternal gaze. The free wind gently rustled the yellowed grass that rolled to the horizon.

His tears finally dried, leaving crimson streaks on his sunken cheeks. He also became aware of drumbeats at the base of the tower. That meant people were nearby. Somehow, Stepan clung to the hope they would help him—at least with water.

Nearby, dry planks creaked, and suddenly two armed men appeared, sabers drawn. They had the look of fierce Sich warriors, yet Stepan recognized neither. Their eyes bore the cold predation of hunters spotting long-awaited prey.

To the sound of decayed stairs groaning beneath their weight and drums growing louder, the strangers led Stepan down a steep ladder. The descent felt eternal until heavy iron doors opened before him. Beyond, amidst swirling gray mist, fires burned in a great circle. Their light flickered on the bare, muscular chests of Cossacks who seemed like fearsome spirits of the beyond in the evening twilight. With precise movements, they pounded an ominous rhythm on massive drums.

To the side, a figure sat on a grand throne constructed of human bones and skulls. Stepan couldn't see the face through the dense fog, but as he approached, he recognized Sirko. On the ataman's broad shoulder sat the familiar rat, greedily nibbling from its master's outstretched hand.

"Ataman, is that you?" Stepan whispered hesitantly, but a sharp blow to his legs from behind forced him to kneel.

"I understand your indignation, my dear friend," Sirko said to the rat. "Of course! This ignoramus wanted to eat you. But don't worry, I won't let anyone harm you."

The rat finished its meal, glanced around with its long snout, squeaked something, and vanished. At a gesture from Sirko, the drumming stopped. Silence fell, and Stepan felt the fresh breath of the Wild Steppe wafting from the darkness beyond the firelit circle.

Sirko stood and approached Stepan. Stepan recoiled as their eyes met. These were not the ataman's eyes. They belonged to some otherworldly being with a void of blackness where a soul should be.

"What have they done to you..." the kharakternyk muttered in despair.

"I am not who you think I am, man," Sirko responded, his piercing gaze unwavering. "I am the great field spirit, the Lord of the Wild Steppe. In dealing with humans, I take a form convenient for you."

Stepan snorted skeptically. Perhaps Sirko had lost his mind—or maybe this truly was the Steppe Spirit, the being of countless childhood tales.

"All kharakternyks who fall in battle against unclean forces pass through me," the spirit continued. "And I decide whether they fade into oblivion or remain eternal guardians of the Steppe."

"So, I'm dead," Stepan said, a sudden clarity lighting his thoughts as if someone had ignited a flame in the darkness. He recalled the fortress, his final conversation with the Turk, his attempt to contact Orysia, and then... Nothing. He couldn't remember the face of the one who killed him.

"Hmm... and what have you decided?" the kharakternyk asked.

The Lord of the Steppe stepped back, and in his hands appeared two sabers from nowhere. Tossing one to Stepan, he said, "Prove yourself a valiant Cossack, and you will become a guardian of the Wild Steppe!"

The Steppe Spirit wielded the weapon with alarming skill. Stepan had to use all his Cossack training just to survive the duel's first moments. The spirit was immune to the magic of kharakternyks; none of Stepan's spells had any effect. Every time they clashed, the spirit held the upper hand.

By the end, Stepan lay exhausted in the dust beneath a drum, his saber cast to the opposite side of the circle. He had no strength left to even lift his head—it felt as though the battle had lasted the entire night. The Lord of the Steppe looked as fresh as if he had just finished breakfast. Dragging Stepan by the leg into the center of the circle, the spirit placed his blade at the kharakternyk's throat.

The drums fell silent again. Stepan thought eternal oblivion might be better than the hellish torments the priests described. But, being dragged through the dust like a sack of refuse was an indignity too far. He was glad his father couldn't see him now. *Soon, it will all be over.*

"Do you know how to recognize a true warrior?" asked the Lord.

"He doesn't drag defeated foes like livestock through the dirt," Stepan retorted bitterly.

"A true warrior doesn't rely solely on muscle or magic," the spirit replied, ignoring the sarcasm. "He gives his soul for victory. None among mortals can defeat me; thus, only true warriors can serve as my guardians."

Stepan sighed wearily.

"And what's your verdict, devil spawn?" he asked irritably.

"You have proven yourself worthy of serving the Wild Steppe!" The blade vanished from the spirit's hand.

"Well, isn't that just grand," Stepan said, rising to his feet.

"But I see in your heart a longing for lost love," the spirit continued. "An eternal life with such a burden would be a torment."

Perched on his throne once more, the Lord stroked the rat that had returned to his lap.

"What are you talking about?" Stepan asked.

"Love for a woman does not suit a Sich warrior," the spirit said. "When he goes to battle, his heart is not fully his own. Such a man cannot serve well as a guardian in my ranks. Yet, you are a skilled fighter, and so I will help you." The soul of your Orysia is searching for you. Go to meet her."

"Where do I go?" Stepan asked gravely.

"My faithful companion will be your guide through the Wild Steppe. Though you sought to eat him, he bears no grudge," said the Lord, gesturing toward the rat.

Chapter Twenty-Seven

"What is this Witch's Path?" asked Petro as he and Myshko saddled their horses.

"The fortune-teller told me it's the path every woman must take if she wishes to become a witch," explained Myshko.

"And a man can walk this path too?"

"Of course, but few men ever return from it. Let's ride. We need to pass through the Gate before dawn breaks on the eastern horizon."

Petro asked no more questions, though he understood little of Myshko's answers. The last time he felt so lost was when Sirko taught him the secrets of the kharakternyk's craft. Yet Sirko's soul had been as clear as a tear on a monkey's cheek. Myshko was different—his eyes were like the still surface of a pond, hiding a treacherous whirlpool beneath the deceptive mirror. Petro couldn't tell whether it was the product of his troubled imagination or if there was real danger. Either way, his choices were limited: either succumb to the torment of haunting visions or trust this stranger and see what happened. Above all, he needed to stay prepared for surprises—and they weren't long in coming.

Petro recognized the place from afar. On the steep bank of a small lake, scattered sawdust from a felled dead tree was still visible. He pulled on the reins.

"What are we doing here?"

Myshko smiled slyly.

"I heard about you from the old hag," he said. "Your dead girl is needed if we are to survive the Witch's Path. You refused to use the power of the mace."

"Are there no living witches left in the Hetmanate?"

"Not one of them would dare return to that path for all the treasures in the world," Myshko explained patiently, tying his horse to a hornbeam tree. "But your Kalyna would happily agree—after all, it's not every day that fools among the living can escort her through the Gate of the Dead."

Petro shot Myshko a suspicious look.

"How do you know all this?"

"Live a month under the same roof as a fortune-teller, and you'll learn even more," Myshko replied cheerfully. He then laid out ritual items on the fresh green grass: a cluster of unripe viburnums and some bones. "Who would've thought—a kharakternyk afraid of a dead girl!"

Kalyna stood barefoot on the dappled surface of the water, wearing the same white blouse Petro had seen her in during his visions. Her dark curly hair cascaded over her thin shoulders, stirring lightly in the breeze. She walked across the water toward the shore as if strolling through a meadow.

But Petro felt neither fear nor loneliness in the face of death as he had when encountered Kalyna in dreams or visions. Instead, the fear in his chest dissipated like morning mist, and he felt strangely light. He was ready to walk toward Kalyna himself, even taking a step, but Myshko grabbed his elbow.

"Don't rush toward death, Cossack. She'll come to you when it's time," Myshko said quietly, keeping his gaze fixed on the apparition.

Kalyna stepped onto the shore and stopped, gazing directly into Petro's eyes.

"I would never disturb your sleep or appear to you in the midst of battle, endangering your life," the girl said. "It is your brother's soul calling you for help. If you don't aid him, he will be doomed to wander forever between the worlds of the living and the dead."

Petro smiled warmly, believing every word that flowed gently from her lips beyond the veil of life.

"Guide us through the Witch's Path," Myshko interjected, "and at the end of the journey, you'll find the peace you long for."

Kalyna turned to him and broke into a bright, ringing laugh.

"Does the esteemed gentleman think that because I am dead, I crave eternal peace? Truly dead are only those who do not love—isn't that right, Petro?"

She turned back to Petro, placing her hands on his shoulders. "Finally, someone has destroyed that cursed tree..." she said with a smile. "I missed you. Did you miss me?"

"Oh-ho!" Myshko exclaimed with a sarcastic smirk. "Look at this! Our nimblest kharakternyk has himself a sweetheart from the beyond. I wonder what the laws of the Sich brotherhood would say about this?"

"I'll do anything for you," Kalyna said. Her lips didn't move, but Petro heard her voice clearly in his mind. "If you want to see me again, come to my grave, pluck a viburnum cluster from the tree, and eat it. I will come to you. These elaborate rituals with bones drain life from the one performing them. And one more thing—be wary of this man; he is dangerous..."

"Doves, shall we get to the point already?" Myshko chimed in again.

Tasawwuf, through the eyes of his host, scrutinized the girl. Her gaze was locked with Petro's. They were silent, but an experienced sorcerer was hard to deceive. Something was happening between the specter and the kharakternyk, but he couldn't discern what. The ritual had drained much of the energy from the body he inhabited, as its previous owner had no connection to magic. This was yet another unexpected complication. Tasawwuf needed Petro's trust, his guard lowered. Only then could he take the young kharakternyk's body and power, claiming the magic of the Sarmatian mace. But first, the phantom had to be dealt with—at the earliest opportunity.

Kalyna turned to Myshko and gifted him with a dazzling smile. "There is nothing simpler than stepping onto the Witch's Path," she said in a mysterious tone. "But are my esteemed guests sure they can walk it and return?"

"Don't worry about us," Myshko replied irritably. "Will you help us?"

"Why not?" the specter answered. "The Gate of the Dead is already waiting."

"And where is it?" Petro asked cautiously, looking around. "There's only open steppe here."

"Petro, can't you see it?" Kalyna asked, surprised.

And Petro saw it.

Chapter Twenty-Eight

"How is this rat supposed to help me?" Stepan asked skeptically as he fastened his scabbard to his wide leather belt.

"He knows the way to the Witch's Path," replied the Lord of the Wild Steppe, stroking his favorite. "And everything he knows; you will know as well."

"I see..." the Cossack muttered.

"Beware and listen carefully to your guide," the spirit advised. "The world of the dead is no less dangerous than the world of the living."

"Care to share what exactly I should be wary of?" Stepan asked, mounting his horse. "I'm not sure I'll understand this... guide."

The Lord pondered briefly before answering.

"Beware the mamuns. They've recently taken to hunting in these parts..."

"I've heard about the Witch's Path from Orysya," Stepan said after hours of silence, addressing the rat clinging to his shirt. "She spoke of it often. But your master didn't say who or what these mamuns[26] are. Do you know?"

The rat clung tightly with its thin claws, staring into the darkness, emitting soft, pitiful squeaks. Stepan sighed. If not for the squeaks and his own breathing, he'd have been enveloped in absolute silence, the cold darkness ink-black around him. Not even the sound of his horse's hooves on the dry steppe grass could be heard.

Eventually, a sliver of yellow moonlight broke through the low clouds, and the dim illumination eased the oppressive weight on Stepan's chest. It made him long for conversation.

"Brother," he muttered, shaking his head, "this isn't going to work. The Field Spirit promised I'd inherit your knowledge, but all you do is squeak. When's dawn here? Feels like we've been riding for a day, and it's still night..."

Suddenly, the rat let out a piercing, unnatural squeal that made Stepan's ears ring before disappearing into the shadows. The Cossack noticed the mist thickening around him, and his horse froze as if rooted to the ground, resisting all coaxing.

Out of nowhere, several female voices began a mournful, haunting song. The mist glowed faintly, and slender shadows began emerging one by one.

Stepan didn't feel fear. He inhaled the thick, smoky air deeply, but along with it seeped a clinging, sticky sorrow. It was as if he

---

[26] Slavic demoness, one of the Slavic fairies

glimpsed something in the mist that he yearned for most, yet it remained out of reach.

For a hardened forty-year-old Cossack, it was an odd sensation: wanting to cry and laugh simultaneously. A strange, almost irresistible urge tempted him to abandon his stubborn horse. He wanted to forget the Witch's Path and Orysiya, lost beneath the vaults of death. He wanted to step into the shimmering mist.

Moments dripped into Stepan's consciousness like thick wild honey into an empty barrel, filling it with cloying numbness. His gnarled fingers released the saber's hilt. He reached for the shadows, desperate as a starving beggar for a nobleman's crumbs.

A sudden flash of lightning blinded him, and for an instant, he saw the rat, standing on its hind legs, squealing shrilly. When the vision vanished, Stepan snapped back to awareness, grasping his weapon once more. The sharp sense of danger burned within him, compelling him to fight.

The shadows solidified into beautiful dark-haired women clad in short black tunics. Each held a massive white feather as if it were a weapon.

Stepan had never fought a woman before, and the prospect unsettled him. Instinctively, he had begun drawing his saber halfway from its scabbard when something sharp and hot touched his neck.

"Surely, in your life, you've slain countless enemies," purred a silky voice behind him, "but this isn't your time."

The voice froze him in place. He dropped his blade in shock. There was no mistake, this was Orysya.

Stepan felt himself sinking again into the mire of suffocating melancholy. Another flash of lightning pulled him free. That voice was an illusion, sorcery, a deception. Orysya waited beyond the Witch's Path, and to reach her, he had to survive.

Frustrated, Stepan thought bitterly how strange it was that even after death, a weary Cossack had to struggle to survive. What of paradise and the heavenly feasts promised by priests?

"You asked the Field Spirit who we are?" came a voice behind him. "We are the mamuns, hunters of human souls…"

In an instant, the warrior-women vanished, and the thick mist transformed into a tornado that hurled Stepan from his horse. A savage, furious wind tore at him, spinning him violently. Each grain of wind-blown sand stung his skin like a swarm of angry bees.

Stepan screamed in agony until unconsciousness claimed him.

It seemed only a moment had passed when he regained awareness, his body a single mass of pain. Opening his swollen eyelids, he saw a young woman in a long black dress. Her dark, luxurious hair was tied neatly at the back of her head. In her hand, she held a feather, tracing its soft tip over Stepan's bloodied face. Her large, dark eyes gleamed with curiosity and perhaps pity.

"What are you staring at? Bring me water," Stepan croaked.

The girl immediately darted away, calling out in an unfamiliar language.

Stepan glanced around. He sat in the middle of a clearing surrounded by pointed tents, tied to the massive trunk of a sprawling oak. Black skies, adorned with a crescent moon, loomed over the eternal night of the steppe. Lamps burned on the ground in a circular pattern, like a string of beads from a mourning tapestry.

Somewhere in the distance, a haunting female chant echoed again, growing louder as it approached. Minutes passed before a procession of women entered the clearing, moving as if floating along the path of lanterns.

They carried a statue of a woman with spread wings and a diamond crown, her face fierce and defiant. In both hands, the statue held long, sharp feathers, her mouth open in an eternal battle cry.

The figure was placed before Stepan, who tried to convince himself it wasn't alive. Yet he couldn't shake the feeling that the stone woman would leap at him at any moment.

The familiar young woman returned, holding a goblet of icy water to his cracked lips.

"I am a priestess of Mamuna, our protector," she said, watching him drink greedily. "Few true warriors enter the Wild Steppe from the land of the living. Most are claimed by the Field Spirit. Capturing someone like you is a rare prize."

"And now what?" Stepan asked wearily.

"We will offer you as a gift to our Lady Mamuna," she replied. "But I will pray that she spares your soul…"

Stepan frowned. "Why the sudden kindness?"

The priestess leaned in close, her voice dropping to a whisper. "Most souls are like flies trapped in a spider's web—easy to drain. But your soul burns with a strange fire. Love has endured even your body's death. I've never seen such a thing. Let us see what the goddess decides."

Then she raised her voice and continued. "Mamuns will kill you as you killed others. But she enjoys prolonging the suffering..."

Alone again, Stepan watched the eerie flames of the lanterns flicker. The wind in the oak's branches sang a mournful dirge.

"Well," thought Stepan, "even in death, a kharakternyk pays the price for his craft."

A squeak broke his reverie. Looking down, he saw the rat, its sharp teeth gnawing through the ropes binding his wrists.

"You're just in time, friend," Stepan muttered, staggering to his feet. "Let's get out of here before these mad women decide otherwise..."

A sharp whistle split the air, and a feathered dart embedded itself in the oak behind him. Its owner, the priestess, stepped forward, her black crystalline eyes glittering with menace.

"Run if you can," she said coldly, "but my sisters will come for you."

Without a second thought, Stepan followed the squealing rat into the shadows.

Chapter Twenty-Nine

Petro felt the foul liquid dripping down his face, yet his broad hands held their prize tightly. If Ivan Rudyi had told him a year ago that his training as a kharakternyk would lead to chasing down a black rooster, Petro Sobol might have reconsidered getting involved in such matters.

Struggling to keep hold of the captured bird, Petro stood in the middle of a cave, ankle-deep in a massive puddle. According to Kalyna, this was where the Gate of the Dead resided, but Petro saw nothing resembling a gate. Only slimy stone vaults covered in a filthy green mold and a stench that could have killed a steppe mouse. The only thing that had caught the kharakternyk's eye upon entering was the rooster, standing perfectly still on one leg in the middle of the cave like a sculpture carved from black granite.

"Well, look at this beauty!" Myskho exclaimed in awe.

"What's to look at?" Petro replied. "I don't know about you, but I'm starving." Without hesitation, he lunged at the rooster.

Catching the bird, however, turned out to be an ordeal. It darted around the cave with incredible speed, forcing Petro to chase it for quite some time before he finally succeeded.

Myskho observed the now mud-smeared kharakternyk with a look of bemused pity. Above, Kalyna's bright laughter echoed through the cave's dark ceilings like a festive song on Kupala Night.

"What's so amusing to her?" Petro wondered. "Is it just because I cut down that cursed tree and burned the rope?"

"Stop looking at me like I've gone mad," Petro grumbled to Myskho. "You'll stop laughing when there's no dry firewood to cook this bird, and Kalyna doesn't know how to roast poultry!"

"Hmm," Myskho replied vaguely; while inwardly noting how desperately the body he inhabited craved sustenance.

"I must warn you, gentlemen," Kalyna said with a laugh, "if you eat that rooster, the Gate of the Dead will remain forever closed."

"And what's the rooster got to do with anything?" Petro asked, disappointed. He looked so comically, wiping mud off his face with the bird's rear that even Myskho couldn't suppress a smile.

"I'll remember this when you're the one in trouble," Petro muttered indignantly.

"Face the wall and let the poor creature go," Kalyna ordered. "Then the Gate will open."

Sighing with regret, Petro released the rooster. Freed, it flapped around the cave before settling back in the middle and letting out an ear-piercing crow.

"Remember this act of mercy, my feathery friend," Petro said, but then noticed something strange.

The water in the puddle began to rise in shimmering droplets, collecting on the surface of one cave wall. Within a minute, the floor was dry, and the wall transformed into a mirror of pure, transparent water.

While Petro and Myskho gaped at the phenomenon, Kalyna approached the mirror with a smile, whispering something. Flames rose from the water, first at the bottom, then to the ceiling. The fire turned the water into an inferno, radiating unbearable heat and the stench of death.

Petro and Myskho recoiled instinctively, but Kalyna nonchalantly declared, "The Gate of the Dead is open."

Petro was far from thrilled. This wasn't how he had envisioned things. "How are we supposed to pass through fire?" Myskho asked in confusion.

In response, the black rooster unexpectedly took flight, vanishing into flames and leaving behind a few charred feathers.

"And where's your bravery gone?" Kalyna teased, laughing at the two men, who stood frozen as if rooted to the spot.

"Fine, I'll go first. Then you can follow—if you dare," she said with a grin.

"It's easy for you to say—you're already dead!" Myskho retorted. "We're still alive, thank God! We'll burn!"

"The line between life and death is an illusion," Kalyna said, her smile fading. "Some of us understand this better than others. Isn't that, right?"

Without waiting for a reply, she turned and stepped into the flames.

"What did she mean by that?" Petro asked.

Myskho shrugged but inwardly acknowledged that Kalyna's ghostly presence was far more dangerous than he had initially thought. Surely, she had long since seen through him. Why hadn't she revealed everything to the kharakternyk yet?

Myskho stepped into the flames first, and Petro followed, squeezing his eyes shut. Emerging on the other side, Petro realized that nothing terrible had happened—aside from slightly signing his topknot. Myskho, however, bore a severe burn on his arm, though he seemed unfazed.

Kalyna stood at the edge of a chasm, staring into the darkness below. Far below, a glowing orange ribbon of molten lava flowed. Across the void, jagged cliffs pierced the low-hanging clouds like knives.

"Where to next?" Myskho asked.

"There," Kalyna said weakly, gesturing toward a wooden bridge disappearing into the gloom. "That's the start of the Witch's Path."

Petro peered over the edge and felt his toes curl. If the ropes couldn't support their combined weight, the fall would be long.

"Why are you standing there? Let's go!" Myskho urged, shoving Petro aside as he stepped onto the rickety boards. Many planks were rotten, crumbling into dust at the slightest touch.

"I'll go last," Kalyna whispered, too softly for Myskho to hear. "I'm already dead, so even if I fall, it won't matter."

The bridge swayed perilously with each step, threatening to send them plunging into the abyss. Stopping was not an option; the lava's searing heat rose from below, making it hard to breathe or think.

Suddenly, something cracked beneath Myskho's foot.

"Careful!" he shouted, but it was too late.

Petro, following close behind, stepped onto the same spot and found himself dangling over the void, gripping a rope with one hand. The bridge groaned and began to give way.

"Kalyna, my love!" he shouted into the void as he let go of the rope. "I'll see you on the other side of life!"

Just as Petro released his grip, an unseen force caught his arm and hauled him back onto the bridge. The first thing he saw was Myskho's flushed face, his eyes blazing with an eerie blue light.

"Hold off on your farewells, lad," Myskho said cheerfully. "We're almost there."

Trying to avoid Kalyna's tearful, frightened eyes, Petro stood and took a few shaky steps forward, finally feeling solid ground beneath his feet.

The bridge ended on a rocky terrace with a small cave. The air here was fresh and warm, carrying the scent of freedom.

"The path is long," Kalyna said, looking around. "I suggest we rest."

"But we need to hurry," Myskho protested.

"There's no need to rush," Kalyna replied. "On the Witch's Path, time doesn't exist. Life and death merge into one, intertwining and flowing into each other. Good and evil don't battle for souls here; everyone decides their own fate."

As she spoke, Petro studied her, and one word hammered in his mind: *witch*. Everything about her—the piercing gaze of her dark eyes, the disheveled hair—spoke of a transformation. How quickly the timid, frightened girl had turned into a true sorceress.

Myskho, too, noticed the changes and didn't argue further. He laid down his coat in the cave and fell into a restless sleep, haunted by memories of a distant past.

Kalyna remained awake, watching the horizon and guarding against the dangers that lay ahead.

Chapter Thirty

The summer evening was fading, one of those warm nights Petro loved most. He remembered returning from the fields with his father, washing off the day's work with sun-warmed water from a large barrel in the yard, and sitting under the awning to wait for dinner. Young cherry trees hummed with beetles, geese splashed noisily in the mud, and his mother clan-ged pots on the veranda. At that moment, Petro felt the peace and joy only a happy child in his family home could know.

Suddenly, the sound of a woman crying, guttural shouts, and the pounding of horse hooves broke the calm. The Tatars had come.

Old Sobol jumped to his feet and rushed into the house to grab his saber and pistols.

"Take your mother and flee to the grove behind the tavern near the pond," he ordered without looking back.

Petro dashed for the door. A sharp whistle passed near his ear, and he saw an arrow piercing his father's thick neck. Blood gurgling, the old man collapsed at his wife's feet. To Petro's astonishment, his mother—usually one for loud laments—offered no cries or tears. Instead, she extended a wea-pon to him, her eyes locked on her son as if she wanted to ask something.

A horseman vaulted over the fence into their yard, brandishing a yataghan, followed closely by another archer. Black arrows struck the doorway near his mother's head, scattering splinters everywhere. Petro managed to shoot the archer—the old man had always kept his pistols loaded and the powder dry. But the rider whipped the second pistol from Petro's hand.

"Run, Mother!" Petro shouted, trying to hold the enemy back. But Sobol's mother didn't move an inch.

More Tatar riders gathered beyond the fence. They waved bloodied yataghans and hurled curses as they watched the scene unfold.

A sharp kick from the rider's boot sent young Sobol crashing against the wall. Smirking cruelly, the Tatar dismounted, clearly relishing the attention of his comrades.

Wiping blood from his forehead, Petro studied his opponent. The face looked familiar, but his dazed mind couldn't place it.

The fight started poorly. Petro kept glancing back at his mother, who stood defiantly on the porch. His enemy pressed relentlessly, tireless and precise. Pinned between the blade and the wall, Petro finally heard the Tatar speak—in Myskho's voice.

"I imagined fighting you many times," he said mockingly. "But I thought you'd be more of a challenge. What about some kharakternyk magic?"

Seizing an opening, Petro counterattacked.

"Though really," the Tatar continued, sneering, "your brother didn't even manage a yelp before he gave me everything I wanted!"

"Who are you?" Petro demanded.

"I hunt the power of the Sarmatian mace," the tasawwuf replied. "Remember how I saved you on that bridge? Now it's your turn to repay me—let me into your body."

"What nonsense is this?" Petro grunted, fending off another strike.

"Your dead witch was sharper than you," the spirit taunted. "She managed to kill Myskho's body, but it didn't suit me—too weak."

Amid the chaos, the fight spilled into the narrow living room. Chairs, tables, pots, and dishes from the cupboard were turned into makeshift weapons. His mother was nowhere to be seen—perhaps she had finally fled.

Suddenly, the Tatar produced a pistol from nowhere.

"Goodbye, boy," he hissed with a sickening grin. "You'll join your mother soon."

The shot rang out, but in that instant, old Sobol's mother materialized out of thin air between them. She felt lifeless to the floor.

With a roar, Petro hurled his saber at the Tatar. The man stared in shock at the hilt protruding from his chest before vanishing into thin air, along with the wrecked remnants of the family home.

When Petro awoke, the first thing he saw was Kalyna's concerned face. At the same time, he felt something sharp and hot against his throat.

"Awake?" Kalyna asked, her voice steely. "Now tell me who you really are."

Petro stared at her in confusion.

"Don't you know me?" he replied irritably. "What kind of joke is this?"

"This is no joke," Kalyna snapped. "You brought a powerful sorcerer into my presence, hidden in someone else's body."

"You mean Myskho?" Petro asked, rubbing his aching head.

"I knew something was wrong the moment I saw him," Kalyna said. "I warned you, but I wasn't certain until just now—when he tried to kill me."

"Then why is that knife at my throat?"

"Because you need to convince me right now that his spirit didn't enter you," Kalyna retorted.

Only then did Petro notice Myskho's body behind her. Its burned face seemed almost alive, one unscathed eye staring straight at him.

"I didn't trust him either," Petro muttered, tearing his gaze away from the corpse.

"Your words aren't enough," Kalyna said coldly.

"What else do you want me to do?"

"Let me into your mind."

"What?!"

"You're a kharakternyk. You know what I mean!"

"A true kharakternyk never lets anyone into his mind," Petro said, searching her eyes for the same dark void he had seen in Myskho's. Sirko had never taught him how to free a soul from foreign enchantments, something Petro now bitterly regretted.

Suddenly, all the events of the past days clicked into place: the first encounter with Myskho and the werewolf skin, the strange conversation at the sorceress's hut, Myskho's uncanny knowledge of the mace and its power. Sirko hadn't destroyed the Turk and had perished himself. The sorcerer had been hunting Petro all along, and he had only harbored vague suspicions. Some kharakternyk he was.

"Don't you trust me?" Kalyna asked, her eyes filling with tears.

"Why would I?" Petro shot back. "You're a ghost. And who's to say that demon isn't in you now?"

"I thought..." Kalyna began, but her voice faltered.

"Next time, think harder before suggesting such nonsense," Petro said curtly.

In a flash, he seized her wrist and twisted until the knife fell from her grasp, clattering to the ground and transforming into a black rooster's feather. Kalyna responded with a resounding slap.

"Let me go, you fool!" she yelled. "I've no luck with men, whether in this world or the next."

"And I seem to attract sorcerers and witches wherever I go," Petro grumbled, picking up the feather.

"You wanted to be a kharakternyk, slicing through ordinary people, huh?" Kalyna retorted sarcastically.

"I don't know what I wanted," Petro admitted. "It just happened..."

"It just happened," she mimicked bitterly. "I've heard that before. All men are the same!"

"Enough," Petro said, trying to placate her. "Tell me, how does this feather turn into a blade?"

"Better throw it away before it gets worse," came a deep voice from nowhere.

Petro drew his saber, and Kalyna picked up the feather, which instantly became a weapon again.

"Restless, aren't you?" the voice sighed wearily.

The next moment, both Petro and Kalyna collapsed unconscious beside Myskho's lifeless body. Around them, pale gray shadows began to gather.

Chapter Thirty-One

A frail, hunchbacked old man, barely taller than a child, crouched down. He had a shiny bald spot and a sharp white beard. He inspected his catch with keen, beady eyes.

"Ah, so you're awake!" he exclaimed gleefully when Kalyna opened her eyes. "Tell your groom to stop pretending he's dead. I can see right through him."

Kalyna glanced worriedly at Petro, but noticing he too was regaining consciousness, she replied coldly, "He's not my groom."

"Well, that's none of my business," the stranger said, brushing off her comment. "I only care about one thing: how did you manage to wander into my domain so perfectly on time?"

"And who are you, old man?" Petro asked, his voice steady.

"I am Okh[27], the Lord of the Dark Crags," he answered, straightening his hunched back. "Typically, those who walk the Witch's Path don't stray from it. They know who I am and what to expect. But it seems I've stumbled upon a pair of utter fools."

---

[27] Okh is a character from Ukrainian folk tales, a cunning ruler of the forest's underground kingdom, a small green old man with a long beard.

"And now what?" Petro asked, glancing around cautiously. They were seated above a pile of fragrant hay inside a spacious tent illuminated by a large firefly in a jar hanging from the ceiling. Surprisingly, they weren't bound.

"If you're wondering about ropes, I have no need for them," Okh said with a sly grin, as if reading Petro's thoughts. "I have very capable guards."

As if to prove his point, two massive, fanged beasts with glowing red eyes materialized before them, resembling wolves but much larger.

"Meet my companions," the old man added smugly.

"What do you plan to do with us?" Kalyna asked. "For your information, I'm dead."

"My dear, I've roamed this world for over a thousand years. I can easily distinguish the dead from the living," Okh said dismissively. "I have no interest in you. My pets only feast on the living..."

"If anything happens to him, I'll turn you into a toad!" Kalyna shot back, leaping to grab Okh by the collar of his worn coat. Surprisingly, the wolf-like creatures didn't react, but the Lord of the Crags burst into a fit of laughter.

"And you claim he's not your groom!"

"I can handle myself," Petro muttered gruffly, embarrassed by her defense.

"You'd have your chance," Okh chuckled, "if not for my old friend, the Lord of the Wild Steppe."

"Do you have to share with him?" Kalyna quipped acidly.

"If you strangle me now, you'll learn nothing," Okh teased.

Reluctantly, Kalyna let go and sat back down, avoiding Petro's gaze, clearly flustered by her outburst.

"Anyway," Okh continued cheerfully, "my eccentric friend recently sent me a messenger along with some dead kharakternyk, asking for help finding the lair of the beautiful Swamp Witch." Suddenly, a rat appeared on Okh's shoulder, squeaking irritably. Ignoring it, Okh went on, "This mortal fool is searching for his beloved witch."

"Stepan?!" Petro exclaimed. "He's alive?"

"Well..." Okh scratched his bald head. "In a sense, yes. Although he was unfortunate enough to fall into the clutches of the mamuns. He barely escaped their deadly embrace, thanks only to my loyal guards."

"Where is he?" Petro demanded, now on his feet and ready to shake the truth out of Okh's ancient bones. "What have you done to him?"

"I saved him," Okh replied with a tinge of disappointment. "Snatched his half-dead soul by the hair before it could slip away..."

"Why would you do that?" Kalyna asked suspiciously. "Do you owe someone a favor?"

Okh turned to her with unexpected seriousness. "Despite my reputation as the cruelest of spirits here, even I wouldn't dare disappoint the Lord of the Wild Steppe. I owe him..."

"Take me to him!" Petro demanded, nearly hitting his head on the tent pole as he stood.

"My, aren't you impatient," Okh said to the rat as he rose. "Don't the living learn to respect their elders anymore?"

They sat together on a rocky ledge, overlooking a chasm that exhaled darkness and cold. Stepan stared at the murky gray blanket of clouds stretching overhead. His eyes, filled with sorrow and longing, seemed to pierce the lifeless sky, seeking the home he'd left behind—his childhood yard, the house, his parents.

Petro scrutinized his brother, carefully listening to his tales of the fortress, Orysya, the Muslim sorcerer, the Wild Steppe spirit, and the mamuns. He tried to absorb every detail, visualizing the events, feeling them as if they were his own. It reminded him of the stories his father used to tell him about the Sich when he was a boy. But something fell off. Perhaps it was because, a living man, he was in the realm of the dead, listening to someone who no longer lived. Or, perhaps it was something within him.

Petro feared admitting the truth: he didn't trust his eyes or ears. The figure before him could be anyone. A hollow emptiness gripped him. What had his kharakternyk path led him to? Death, distrust, and isolation. Was this what life was supposed to be? Was it worth it?

"Why didn't that Turkish sorcerer possess you?" Petro finally asked, embarrassed by the question. He felt as though Stepan could see his doubt.

"I don't know," Stepan answered simply.

Silence followed—thick, sticky, unnatural between brothers who had found each other despite death.

"What did Father say about me?" Stepan asked, still gazing at the clouds.

"He said you were a scout and died fighting the Tatar garrison at Perekop."

"That was a lie. Sirko ordered the rumors spread so I could move safely through Kazykermen."

"I've grown used to lies lately..." Petro muttered.

"I understand your mistrust, given all you've faced," Stepan said, looking Petro directly in the eyes. It was a look Petro remembered from childhood when Stepan would try to coax a confession about stolen cherries from the neighbor's yard. Shame washed over Petro.

"You're alive, and I'm dead," Stepan continued. "There's no path back for me, but you can return. Live a good life for both of us. Avenge our parents, our home, our village."

"I'll return when you find peace," Petro said softly.

Stepan smiled. "You were a terrible liar as a child, and you haven't improved."

"What's that supposed to mean?"

"Admit it—you came to the underworld chasing the skirt of a dead girl, didn't you?"

"You don't seem to sit still in the underworld either," Petro retorted.

Stepan laughed. "If we were alive, you'd be mad at me."

"This isn't life," Petro replied quietly, "and I'm not the same."

"Tell me more about Father and Mother…"

After hours of riding a shaggy beast down winding mountain paths, Petro's legs and backside ached terribly. The creature, resembling a massive wolf, looked sturdy but felt like skin and bones beneath its dirty fur.

Kalyna sat behind him, her arms wrapped tightly around his waist, her head resting on his shoulder as she dozed. What did a dead girl dream about? Petro tried not to move, afraid to disturb her, though it was difficult on Oh's peculiar mount. The feeling of her hair brushing his face was oddly comforting…

One question haunted him: What had Oh meant when he called Petro, her groom? Was the malicious spirit mocking them, or did Kalyna truly care for him? And if she didn't, why did it matter so much to him?

His father once said that a woman's love was like a wild beast—a real man had to tame it.

Stepan, riding ahead, suddenly stopped. He dismounted and approached Petro.

"Oh's guardians won't go any further," Stepan said. "We're at the edge of the Swamp Witch's domain."

Petro surveyed the flatlands they had reached after another mountain pass. The valley, surrounded by dark, jagged peaks, was covered in a vibrant yellow-green carpet of spurge and marsh marigold.

Mist hovered above the ground, veiling the black patches of boggy mud.

"There's nothing here," Petro said, puzzled.

"The Lord of the Wild Steppe said the local spirits despise visitors. We'll be noticed soon," Stepan replied.

"Are you sure Orysya is here?" Petro asked doubtfully.

"Every dead witch ends up in the Swamp Witch's domain," Kalyna murmured, her voice soft but firm. "She makes them hide in the bogs, luring young men to their doom. She won't give up Orysya easily, Stepan."

"Why not?" he asked warily.

"Okh said she's too greedy for human souls…"

Chapter Thirty-Two

Petro draped his cloak over Kalyna's frail shoulders and sat beside her. They sat silently for a long time, staring into the eternal twilight of the realm of the dead.

"Tell me, Petro, what will happen when Stepan and Orysya are reunited?" Kalyna asked.

"They'll return to the Steppe," Petro replied, "and perhaps ask the Lord of the Wild Steppe to send their souls into oblivion."

"And what about you?"

Petro flinched. He'd been asking himself that same question ever since meeting Stepan.

"Is there any way for both of us to return to the world of the living?"

Kalyna gave him a tender look.

"When the dead return to the living, nothing good ever comes of it."

"Then I'll stay here with you..."

Kalyna scooted closer and rested her head on Petro's strong shoulder. Her hair brushed against his cheek, soft and comforting.

"Our love is strange, Petro," she said after a long silence. "No declarations, no passion. It's as if we're one, and then suddenly, like a veil is lifted, there's an impenetrable wall between us.

"You mean distrust?" Petro ventured, daring to pull her closer.

"No, I mean death. Even when you're here with me, it's always there, between us."

"Then I'll die to be with you!"

"Are you mad?"

"Stepan could've served the Lord of the Wild Steppe as a guardian," Petro explained heatedly, "but he risked his soul to be united with Orysya for eternity. Why should I be any different?"

"You have obligations in the world of the living—to your brother and your parents."

"Am I so loathsome to you that you're eager to get rid of me?" Petro asked sadly.

"I wish I could always be with you," Kalyna whispered, pressing herself closer to him.

"Did you see that?" Petro suddenly asked.

"See what?"

"Look, over there!"

Kalyna rubbed her sleepy eyes. She saw brightly colored lights flitting across the valley, as if to welcome important guests. More appeared with every passing moment.

"Are those fireflies?" Stepan's voice came from behind them.

"Do fireflies come in such colors?" Petro wondered aloud.

"That's how the Swamp Witch greets us," Kalyna said quietly, trembling.

"Don't be afraid," Petro tried to comfort her. "I'm here with you."

"The Swamp Witch is the powerful patroness of all witches. "This is where the Witch's Path ends," Kalyna said, her voice shaking. Terror swept through her, leaving her breathless and paralyzed.

"Isn't this what you wanted?" Petro asked, puzzled, watching the lights multiply and draw closer.

"To become a witch, a woman must confront her deepest fear," Kalyna said, her teeth chattering. "Only then can extraordinary powers awaken within her."

"And if she can't?" Stepan asked.

"She drowns in these swamps and remains forever alone with her awakened terror…"

Kalyna opened her mouth to say more but froze. Her eyes grew wide, sweat beaded on her brow, and she clutched Petro, screaming. Her piercing cry sent chills down both Sobol brothers' spines. Along with the scream, translucent streams of anguish and pain poured out of her, accumulated over years in the darkest corners of her soul.

Her terror erupted with an overwhelming force, tearing at her consciousness. Kalyna pushed Petro away, rolling on the ground, tearing at her hair and scratching her face, neck, and chest until they bled.

The Sobol tried to stop her, but the fear gave her superhuman strength, and she flung the two strong men aside like rag dolls.

Petro drew his saber and charged into the swarm of "fireflies," shouting, "Stop!!!"

He swung his blade wildly, trying to disperse them. They retreated briefly but then surged back, clinging to his boots and the dew-wet steel like leeches.

"Stop!!!" he roared again, but his voice, raw and hoarse, was swallowed by the storm of Kalyna's terror.

Suddenly, everything ceased. A deafening silence rang in his ears, as if the world itself had held its breath. Kalyna, coughing up blood, tried to rise. A stunned Stepan helped her to her feet.

The air was unnaturally clear now. Breathing heavily, Petro looked around. About ten steps away, a tall blonde woman in a long, translucent gown stood on the swamp. Her head was adorned with a crown that sparkled with shifting gemstones.

"The Swamp Witch..." Kalyna whispered weakly.

"In your world, my sisters are tortured and killed," the woman's voice echoed over the swamp, "but here, no weapon can harm them."

"I haven't killed anyone yet," Petro retorted, "though I'm tempted!"

"These lights are the souls of dead witches."

Petro sheathed his saber and stepped back. The "fireflies" clustered around the Swamp Witch. One began to grow rapidly. It became a blinding sphere of light. From it, a woman emerged, stepping forward with deliberate grace.

"Orysya!" Stepan cried, rushing toward her, only to collide with an invisible barrier. Dropping to his knees, he reached out with both hands.

"Orysya, it's me, Stepan!" he called, his voice breaking with emotion. For the first time, Petro saw tears on his brother's stern face.

"She doesn't remember you," the Swamp Witch said, her voice void of emotion. "But I know why you're here."

"Then release my beloved to me," Stepan pleaded, "for I'll never have peace until our souls are reunited..."

"In this swamp, as in the world of the living, everything has a price," she replied.

"I'll pay anything!"

Stepan knelt before Orysya as if praying to the Virgin Mary. But the dead witch remained indifferent, her cold gaze fixed beyond him, staring into the surrounding darkness.

It hurt Petro to see his brother like this. Where was the proud, unyielding warrior he had always admired? Had his strength been a mask, hiding a different man? Could a woman, even a witch, reduce a true kharakternyk to this?

But what did Petro know of the power women held over men's souls? No wonder the Sich had forbidden women for centuries. Looking at the Swamp Witch's impassive face and his brother's humiliation, Petro finally understood the wisdom of that rule.

Rage bubbled in his chest. He wanted to charge at the Swamp Witch with his saber, but Kalyna's cold fingers lightly grasped his hand, holding him back.

"You have nothing of value," the Swamp Witch said, "but your brother does..."

Stepan tore his gaze away from Orysya and looked at Petro.

"Listen to me, swamp hag," Petro snapped. "If you need a life, take mine. Just don't choke on it!"

The Swamp Witch's deathly visage twisted into a smirk. "Living men in the realm of the dead are always intriguing," she mused, her voice like frost in a crypt. "Passion, pain, guilt, hatred—all of it is like a cold wind cutting through a suffocating tomb."

"Make your decision!" Petro demanded.

"Surrendering your life for your brother's would make you feel like a hero," the Swamp Witch said. "After all, in your family, Stepan was always the respected warrior, fighting alongside your father. Unlike you, the boy your mother hid under her skirts, trying to keep your wild Cossack spirit in check. And for that maternal weakness, you secretly hated your brother, even if you didn't realize it yourself."

"You're lying, you cursed phantom!" Petro choked out, but his trembling lips betrayed him. He felt exposed, raw. He wanted to hide from Stepan, from Orysya, from the Swamp Witch's piercing gaze—even Kalyna's eyes seemed to reflect disappointment.

"How does it feel to see the dark corners of your soul reflected in the eyes of those you love, and to hate them for it?"

When red anger clouded Petro's vision, and a primal scream was ready to escape him, Kalyna's voice rang out.

"Enough!"

"Those were the words I told my sisters when they tried to kill your groom," the Swamp Witch said. "Remember our first meeting on these swamps, Petro, when you were searching for Orysya? If I'd wanted your death, you'd already be dead. Don't hate the one who reveals the truth—it is a gift."

"My soul for Orysya's," Kalyna said softly, stepping forward.

Before Petro could react, the invisible barrier swallowed her. At the same time, Orysya collapsed into Stepan's arms, unconscious.

"Kalyna!"

"Farewell, my love," her voice echoed faintly. "Death has separated us forever, but we will always be together."

Petro screamed curses and slammed his fists, his saber, and his whole body against the unseen wall, trying to break through.

Kalyna stood just beyond his reach, her tear-streaked face growing colder, her eyes hollow and empty.

And then, everything disappeared. Darkness returned, tasting of swamp water.

"Farewell, brother," Stepan said quietly. Holding Orysya, he faded into the shadows.

Petro left alone a living man in the realm of the dead.

Epilogue

All the cemeteries in the Hetmanate share the same somber face, adorned with crooked crosses etched by the unforgiving hand of time. Each gravestone resembles a scroll where the illiterate hand of fate reluctantly scribbles its meager mark.

The sound of shod hooves thudded against the ground, reverberating as if beneath the green blanket of grass lay a void—the final refuge for the dead.

Petro reined in his horse and glanced around, searching for someone. The old cemetery stretched endlessly before him. Its graves were crowded together, forming an uneven line that vanished into the dark crimson horizon of the evening sky.

Near one grave without a cross, Petro spotted a small, hunched figure. From afar, it seemed as if Death herself had come to visit one of her wards. He dismounted and approached.

"She was buried here in secret so the priest wouldn't find out," rasped the voice of the old soothsayer.

"After all, she was a suicide." Petro crouched beside the grave and sat in silence for a long time. He stared intently at the damp earth, as if trying to see through it to the familiar face that lay beneath.

"That man never returned?" the old woman asked, sighing heavily. "Now I'm left without a storage shed..."

"I'll fix your shed for you, grandmother," the kharakternyk replied. "

Printed in Dunstable, United Kingdom